Sunny

**Other books by
Ann M. Martin**

Leo the Magnificat
Rachel Parker, Kindergarten Show-off
Eleven Kids, One Summer
Ma and Pa Dracula
Yours Turly, Shirley
Ten Kids, No Pets
Slam Book
Just a Summer Romance
Missing Since Monday
With You and Without You
Me and Katie (the Pest)
Stage Fright
Inside Out
Bummer Summer

THE KIDS IN MS. COLMAN'S CLASS series
BABY-SITTERS LITTLE SISTER series
THE BABY-SITTERS CLUB mysteries
THE BABY-SITTERS CLUB series
CALIFORNIA DIARIES series

California Diaries #2

Sunny

Ann M. Martin

SCHOLASTIC INC.
New York   Toronto   London   Auckland   Sydney

The author gratefully acknowledges
Peter Lerangis
for his help in
preparing this manuscript.

ISBN 0-590-29836-4

12 11 10 9 8 7 6 5 4 3 2 1   7 8 9/9 0 1/0

Printed in the U.S.A   40

First Scholastic printing, August 1997

MONDAY 10/20
12:15 A.M.

I HATE MY LIFE.

DESPISE IT.

I WOULD TRADE IT IN A MINUTE FOR ANYONE ELSE'S.

THAT'S ALL I HAVE TO SAY.

GOOD NIGHT.

TUESDAY 10/21
1:06 A.M.

BACK AGAIN, SAME PLACE, DIFFERENT DAY.

SAME LIFE, TOO. UNFORTUNATELY.

MISERABLE.

HATEFUL.

POINTLESS.

SLEEPLESS.

NIGHT THREE OF INSOMNIA. I CANNOT BELIEVE IT. THE VERY LAST THING I NEED.

I'VE LISTENED TO ALL MY CDs. I'VE EVEN TRIED DOING HOMEWORK, BUT THAT JUST MADE ME EVEN MORE DEPRESSED.

I ACTUALLY THOUGHT ABOUT CALLING DAWN.

For about a second. Like, she would really be thrilled to hear me at this hour, complaining about the same old stuff.

So I'll just sit here and do something that would make my teachers faint.

Write. Voluntarily.

Maybe I'll bore myself to sleep.

Dawn used to say my name fit my personality. Sunny. The sunny Sunny Winslow.

I hate that. It's so wrong.

Well, it does feel better to write this out. These journals aren't such a stupid idea after all. Okay, let's hit all the problems, from the top.

Number one. I am very upset about Mom. Three days ago I told her to call Dr. Merwin about her wheezing. I didn't like the way she sounded. Of course, she waited until today, when she's really sick. So now she has to go back to the hospital for observation. Plus she has to stop chemotherapy and radiation treatments until she's better.

Number two. Dad. When the renovations in his store began, he became the Control Freak of the Century. This is his life now:

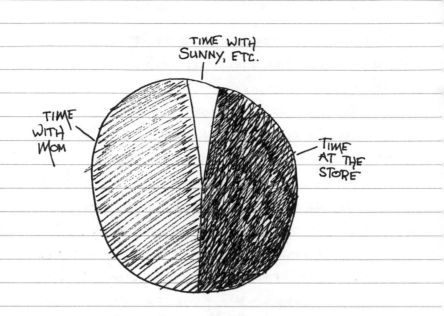

TIME WITH
SUNNY, ETC.

TIME
WITH
MOM

TIME
AT THE
STORE

MOST OF "ETC." IS TAKEN UP WITH SLEEP.

WHICH DAD HAS NO TROUBLE WITH. I CAN
HEAR HIM SNORING IN THE NEXT ROOM. HE SOUNDS
LIKE WOOD SHOP. I DON'T KNOW HOW MOM PUTS
UP WITH IT. I DON'T KNOW HOW I PUT UP WITH
IT.

I'LL JUST STAY AWAKE, THAT'S ALL. AT SCHOOL
TOMORROW I'LL LOOK LIKE A HORROR MOVIE. SUNNY
THE UNDEAD. MAGGIE AND DAWN WILL GIVE ME
MORE USELESS INSOMNIA TIPS.

LIKE TODAY. MAGGIE SUGGESTED I SHOULD
LOOK OUT THE WINDOW AND PICK OUT
CONSTELLATIONS. WELL, I DON'T KNOW HOW MANY

STARS SHE CAN SEE THROUGH THE PALO CITY SMOG. THE ONES I SAW ALL LOOKED LIKE THE BIG DIPPER.

DAWN? SHE HAD INSOMNIA TOO, OVER "THE CHANGES WE'RE FACING." WHICH I GUESS MEANS THE EIGHTH-GRADERS' SWITCH FROM THE MIDDLE SCHOOL TO THE HIGH SCHOOL BUILDING. I DON'T UNDERSTAND DAWN SOMETIMES. SHE'S STILL MY BEST FRIEND BUT HELLO? I MEAN, WE'RE THIRTEEN. WE BELONG WITH THE OLDER KIDS. ESPECIALLY THE GUYS. OKAY, WE DON'T "RULE." OKAY, HIGH SCHOOL KIDS LURED US TO THAT PARTY AT MS. KRUEGER'S EMPTY HOUSE, JUST TO GET US IN TROUBLE. BUT ONLY SOME OF THEM DID. MOST OF THE OTHERS SEEM PRETTY COOL. LIKE DUCKY. ANYWAY, CONSIDER THE ALTERNATIVE. WHO WANTS TO HANG WITH TEDDY BEAR HUGGERS AND GIGGLE OVER SQUEAKY-VOICED BOYS?

MAYBE JILL DOES. HONESTLY, THAT GIRL REALLY MAKES ME SICK. I'M GLAD MAGGIE AND DAWN AND I HAVE DRIFTED AWAY FROM HER.

IF ANY OF MY FRIENDS -- ANY OF THEM, EVEN DAWN -- READ THIS, THEY'D FALL OVER. THEY THINK I'M SO CONFIDENT. SO TOGETHER. (WELL, MAYBE NOT TOGETHER. THEY SAW ME HURL CHUNKS AT THAT PARTY. NOT EXACTLY A TOGETHER THING TO DO.)

Sometimes I think I'm the only eighth-grader at Vista who tries to have any fun at all. Which is totally ironic, considering my frame of mind. I think the move turned everyone into zombies.

Including Maggie, who used to be so cool. That's ancient history. She refused to cut math with me today. And she was so freaked out when I had my navel pierced. Dawn was too, but I kind of expected that. (Jill, of course, almost fainted, which makes it so much fun to flash my ring at her in the school hallways.)

I don't know why I even bother trying to show signs of life. Nobody appreciates it. Everybody is mad at me for something. It's not just Dawn and Maggie, either. Dad's being a pain too. He keeps telling me I should be more serious. And all my teachers think I'm a slacker.

I know. I should start wearing plaid wool skirts, stop painting my fingernails black, join the math club, and discuss global politics at lunch. I mean, life is hard enough. PEOPLE SHOULD LIGHTEN UP, in my humble opinion.

I just yawned. That's a good sign.

I AM BORING MYSELF TO SLEEP.

JUST AS WELL. MY FINGERS ARE STARTING TO
HURT. I HAVE NEVER WRITTEN THIS MUCH IN MY
LIFE.

WEDNESDAY MORNING 10/22

I JUST READ WHAT I WROTE YESTERDAY.

I'M GLAD I'M NOT MY FRIEND. I WOULD DRIVE
ME CRAZY.

MOM AND DAD JUST PASSED BY ON THEIR WAY
DOWNSTAIRS TO BREAKFAST. MOM WAS YELLING AT
DAD FOR NOT HOLDING ONTO HER ENOUGH. SHE
SEEMS SO ANGRY.

WELL, SHE'S ALLOWED. SHE'S ALLOWED TO BE
MAD AT THE WORLD. I WOULD BE, IF I HAD LUNG
CANCER. (ACTUALLY, I AM MAD, AT THE TOBACCO
COMPANIES.)

SHE'S ALSO DEPRESSED ABOUT GOING TO THE
HOSPITAL. FOR TWO DAYS SHE HAS NOT WORN HER
WIG. SHE SAYS SHE'S TOO TIRED TO PUT IT ON.
SHE WEARS A KERCHIEF INSTEAD, TO COVER HER
THINNING HAIR. SHE SAYS IT WILL ALL GROW BACK
WHEN THE CHEMOTHERAPY ENDS. I CAN'T WAIT. NOT
THAT THE HAIR MATTERS. I MEAN, I'D TAKE MOM

BALD AND BEARDED IF SHE WERE HEALTHY AGAIN.
IT'S JUST THAT <u>NOT</u> WEARING A WIG SEEMS LIKE
SOME KIND OF SIGNAL. AS IF MOM IS STARTING
TO GIVE UP.

MAYBE I'M THINKING ABOUT IT TOO MUCH.
MAYBE SHE <u>IS</u> JUST TIRED. BESIDES, WEARING THAT
WIG MUST BE LIKE HAVING A THICK OLD HAT ON
ALL DAY. WOULD I DO IT? NO WAY. KERCHIEFS FOR
ME, BABY.

HAVE I MENTIONED I HATE PUBLIC BUSES?
I HATE PUBLIC BUSES!!!!!!!!
THERE. I MENTIONED IT.

I AM ON ONE RIGHT NOW, GOING TO VISIT
MOM IN THE HOSPITAL. THE DRIVER IS EVIL. JUST
TO ANNOY US RIDERS, HE IS AIMING FOR EVERY
SINGLE POTHOLE ON NARANJA BOULEVARD. I THINK
HE WANTS TO GET US ALL SICK.

IT'S LUNCH PERIOD. I SHOULD BE SITTING IN
THE AIR-CONDITIONED CAFETERIA OF VISTA WITH ALL
THE OTHER EIGHTH-GRADERS. INSTEAD, I'M SWEATING
LIKE A PIG, BOUNCING DOWN THE STREET ON A

PUBLIC ROLLER COASTER AS I SIT BEHIND A FAT MAN IN A HAWAIIAN SHIRT EATING A TUNA SALAD SANDWICH. A LOT OF IT IS ACTUALLY <u>ON</u> THE SHIRT, BLENDING IN NICELY WITH THE DESIGN. WHY DOES TUNA TASTE SO GOOD BUT SMELL SO AWFUL?

HERE'S THE HOSPITAL. GOT TO GO.

WEDNESDAY AFTERNOON

I'M IN SOCIAL STUDIES NOW. MR. HACKETT THINKS I AM WRITING A REPORT ON FEDERAL ELECTIONS. I WILL, LATER.

NOTE TO ME -- WATCH ELECTION VIDEO TONITE!!!!

BUT I CAN'T THINK ABOUT POLITICS NOW. I HAVE TO WRITE ABOUT WHAT'S IMPORTANT.

I HAD THE WEIRDEST HOSPITAL VISIT. I AM STILL RECOVERING FROM IT.

FIRST OF ALL, AS I WALKED IN, THE RECEPTIONIST WAS DOING A CROSSWORD PUZZLE. WHEN I SAID "WINSLOW," SHE MUST HAVE THOUGHT I WAS GIVING HER A CLUE, BECAUSE SHE KEPT ON WRITING. I PRACTICALLY HAD TO YELL IN HER EAR TO GET HER ATTENTION.

After that start, I was sent off through about 5 miles of corridors. They build a new wing in that hospital every week, just to torment visitors. I love walking around in public places, staring into rooms full of sick strangers, with Duh all over my face.

Anyway, when I got to Mom's room, she wasn't there.

Her bed was empty. Dad was sitting next to it, with the phone cradled to his ear. He was practically hysterical. "What do you mean, they've already started digging?" he yelled.

Digging?

I almost fell over. I mean, my knees were actually weak. I guess hearing that question, and seeing Mom's empty bed, and my crazy frame of mind -- it all made me think that

I don't even want to write what I thought. It's too morbid.

I sat in a green vinyl chair next to the bed and tried to look calm, while I listened to Dad arguing with someone who was not me (for a change).

The "digging" was no big deal. Well, I guess it was for Dad. A new bookstore's

PLANNING TO OPEN A COUPLE OF BLOCKS AWAY FROM HIS. SOME BULLDOZERS ARE DIGGING A FOUNDATION.

DAD WAS STRESSING ABOUT HOW THE COMPETITION WAS GOING TO "RUIN HIM." I KNOW I SHOULD HAVE BEEN CONCERNED TOO, BUT I WASN'T. I WAS THERE TO SEE MOM.

WHEN THE ORDERLY FINALLY WHEELED HER IN, SHE WAS SMILING.

HERE'S THE WEIRD THING. SMILES ARE SUPPOSED TO MAKE YOU FEEL GOOD, RIGHT? WELL, I TOOK ONE LOOK AT MOM'S EXPRESSION AND ALMOST BURST INTO TEARS. I WAS SO SHOCKED, I ACTUALLY GASPED.

GREAT, SUNNY. REALLY SUAVE. I MEAN IMAGINE HOW SHE FELT. IT'S LIKE HAVING SOMEONE LOOK AT YOUR FACE AND CRY OUT, "EWWWWW!"

BUT I COULDN'T HELP IT. MOM LOOKED TERRIBLE. LIKE A TIME-LAPSE IMAGE OF HERSELF GROWING OLDER BEFORE MY EYES. HOW DID SHE GET AGE SPOTS ON HER SCALP? SHE'S ONLY 42! AND WHAT HAPPENED TO HER ARMS? THEY USED TO BE SO THICK AND MUSCLEY FROM ALL THOSE YEARS OF POTTERY. NOW THE SKIN SORT OF SAGS OFF THEM.

I MEAN, I SAW HER AT HOME ONLY THIS MORNING. SHE DIDN'T LOOK NEARLY AS BAD THEN.

Am I overreacting? I must have been overreacting. The fluorescent lights in the hospital are harsh. (Even my skin looked a little green.) Plus Mom was not wearing any makeup -- or a wig or kerchief, for that matter. I'm still not used to seeing Mom totally natural like that. And she's been sick.

Still, seeing her smile was depressing. Like watching a flower trying to grow through the wreckage of an old building. (Not that Mom looks like an old building. I just mean -- oh, I know what I mean. WHY AM I MAKING EXCUSES TO MYSELF?)

Mom could tell right away I was upset. "Are you all right, sweetheart?" she asked.

"Fine," I said. "Just hay fever."

I mean, ridiculous excuse or what?

Anyway, the orderly, Dad, and I helped Mom into bed. She tried to wave us all off. She said she was feeling much better, "strong as an ox." I noticed for the first time a big plate of fruit on her night table, but she hadn't touched it.

"Shouldn't you eat, Mom?" I asked.

"I will," she said. But she didn't. Instead,

SHE ASKED DAD ABOUT THE STORE. SINCE HE DIDN'T WANT TO UPSET HER, HE PRETENDED EVERYTHING WAS FINE, NERVOUSLY PICKING AT THE FRUIT PLATE. SINCE HE'S SUCH A BAD ACTOR, MOM KEPT SAYING, "NO, REALLY, PAUL, ARE YOU SURE?" WHILE DAD KEPT TRYING TO CHANGE THE TOPIC.

I FELT LIKE A PIECE OF FURNITURE. I DIDN'T KNOW WHAT TO SAY. SO I JUST SAT THERE.

MY EYES KEPT WANDERING OVER TO THE FRUIT PLATE. MY STOMACH BEGAN RUMBLING.

THEN I THOUGHT ABOUT LUNCH. AND I GLANCED AT MY WATCH.

I NEARLY JUMPED OUT OF MY SEAT. LUNCH PERIOD WAS OVER. I DIDN'T MIND, BUT I WAS AFRAID MOM WOULD FREAK.

"UH, I HAVE TO GO!" I BLURTED OUT.

"OH, DEAR," MOM SAID. "I'M KEEPING YOU FROM SCHOOL."

"NO, I KEPT MYSELF!" I SAID, EDGING TO THE DOOR. "I MEAN, I WANTED TO. I'M GLAD I VISITED. BUT I HAVE TO --"

"DO THEY STILL HAVE TRUANT OFFICERS THESE DAYS?" DAD ASKED. I MEAN, COME ON.

"I CAN WRITE YOUR TEACHER A NOTE," MOM SAID, REACHING FOR HER GLASSES ON THE NIGHT TABLE.

"That's okay. Really." I was already in the open doorway. Holding the doorknob. Racing away from Mom, having said barely a word to her.

Some visit. I felt so guilty.

"I'll come back," I vowed. "Tomorrow. After school."

Zoom. I ran down the hallway.

I almost collided with Dr. Merwin, who was bustling around the corner. He didn't even notice me. His face was buried in a manila folder.

I watched him stride into Mom's room. "Hello, Mr. and Mrs. Winslow," he said softly. "I, uh, have the latest radiology report."

Forget lunch. Something was up. I had to hear this. I tiptoed back to the room and stood just outside the door.

"As you can see here," Dr. Merwin's voice rumbled to the sound of rustling papers, "the spread seems to be holding firm, and the lungs are clearing. All good news."

Hope, hope hope . . .

"But," he continued, "as you suspected, we are showing a lump of some sort in the region of the clavicle."

"OH, DEAR," MOM MURMURED.

"WHAT KIND OF LUMP?" DAD ASKED.

"WE'LL DO A BIOPSY," DR. MERWIN REPLIED. "IT IS NOT IN A ZONE WE USUALLY CONSIDER SUSPECT, BUT WE NEED TO CHECK IT OUT ANYWAY. . . ."

THAT WAS ALL I COULD STAND TO HEAR. I BOLTED AWAY.

A LUMP. MOM HAS ANOTHER LUMP.

I SHOULD NEVER, NEVER BE OPTIMISTIC.

HOPE IS A DISEASE.

WEDNESDAY NIGHT

WHY ARE ALL MY TEACHERS DORKS?

WHILE I WAS WRITING THAT LAST ENTRY, MR. HACKETT WAS PEERING OVER MY SHOULDER. I LOOKED UP AND THERE HE WAS, WITH HIS CHEESY GRIN AND HIS NOSTRIL HAIRS HANGING OUT. HE NEARLY SCARED ME TO DEATH.

"SO, SUNNY," HE SAID CHEERFULLY, "WHAT DISCOVERIES HAVE YOU MADE ABOUT THE RELEVANCE OF THE ELECTORAL COLLEGE IN THE MODERN POLITICAL PROCESS?"

OR SOMETHING LIKE THAT.

I pulled myself together. "What college?" I asked.

I thought that was a reasonable question, but Janice Branford started snickering behind me. Her shadow, Dustin Schmidt, joined in, along with one or two others.

"Electoral," Mr. Hackett said dryly. "You know, what we've been talking about for the last half hour?"

"Oh, _that_ college!" I blurted out. "Sure. I mean, I think it's very important to teach the voters . . . about who's running and all."

Mr. Hackett was not pleased. "Please stay after class, would you, Sunny?"

More snickering. All from behind me. (People are so brave when you can't see them.)

I was furious. But it was near the end of class, so I had no chance to get back at anyone. I stayed after and Mr. Hackett gave me a lecture about paying attention. He said he was "concerned about my level of participation." He didn't give me a chance to speak for the longest time. Finally he asked, "Why _were_ you late, anyway?"

"My mom is dying of cancer," I said, "and I had to visit her in the hospital."

As if he didn't know, I thought. I mean, he had just snooped in my personal journal.

But he looked as if I'd just punched him. The color drained from his face. "Oh, my . . ." he said. "I -- I knew she was sick, but I . . . well, I can see how you'd be distracted, of course."

"Yeah," I murmured.

Mr. Hackett stood up. Now he had this soft, pitying, superconcerned expression. "Well. If I can, uh, be of any help . . ."

"Thanks," I said.

I rose from my chair and left.

I took the long way to math, past the gym, where fewer people would see me.

I was mortified. Absolutely mortified. Dying of cancer? How could I have said those words? How could I have used Mom like that? La-di-da, just another convenient alibi, right up there with "My dog ate my homework" and "I had a stomachache."

AAAAAAGH!

Stupid. I am so stupid.

I just know Mr. Hackett's going to want a family conference. And in the meantime, he's

GOING TO BLAB TO ALL THE OTHER TEACHERS
ABOUT WHAT I SAID.

THAT IS THE LAST THING I NEED. I KNOW
THE TEACHERS ARE AWARE THAT MOM'S SICK, BUT
NONE OF THEM KNOWS HOW BAD SHE REALLY IS.

AND HOW BAD IS SHE? I DON'T EVEN KNOW.
ONE DAY SHE LOOKS WELL, THE NEXT SHE'S WEAK
AND FRAIL. THE TREATMENTS ARE STRENGTHENED,
THE TREATMENTS ARE WEAKENED. ONE NIGHT SHE'S
COUGHING AND WHEEZING, THE NEXT SHE SLEEPS LIKE
A BABY.

I DON'T MIND CONFIDING IN DAWN OR
MAGGIE, BUT I DON'T WANT THE WHOLE SCHOOL
ASKING QUESTIONS. OR LOOKING AT ME AS IF I'M
SOME HELPLESS, PITIFUL SOUL.

THIS IS NOT A PUBLIC AFFAIR.

HONESTLY, I AM SO SICK OF ALL THIS.

I AM SICK OF . . .

HOSPITAL VISITS.

HAIR IN THE SINK.

MEDICINES ALL OVER THE HOUSE.

KNOW-IT-ALL DOCTORS WHO ARE ALWAYS WRONG.

RUNNING OUT TO THE DRUGSTORE ALL THE TIME.

NOT BEING ABLE TO LEAVE HOME ON WEEKENDS
BECAUSE MOM CAN'T TRAVEL.

visitors who act as if they're paying last respects and cry as they drive away in the car.

I DO NOT NEED THIS.

If I keep my chin up and act happy, I feel guilty. If I worry too much, I lose sleep.

I need to get away, do something fun. But can I? No. Our big trip to Lake Tahoe, which we planned for months? Postponed when Mom got sick. My big blowout party at our house for all my friends? Canceled.

"We have to put things on hold," Dad says, "until we know more about Mom. Just be patient."

Well, that's easy for him to say. He has the store. It's his life.

But hello, what about MY life? I'm supposed to have one too.

I feel as if someone is standing over me with a remote, pressing the PAUSE button.

I keep waiting for things to get back to normal. But sometimes I think that's a stupid idea. I don't know what normal is anymore. When I think of the future, my mind turns into soup. Will Dad and I move to a smaller

HOUSE? WILL HE TOTALLY FREAK OUT? WILL HE
START DATING? WILL I HAVE TO TAKE A JOB IN
HIS STORE, OR LEARN TO DO THE BILLS AND MAKE
DINNERS THE WAY MOM DOES?

HONESTLY, SOMETIMES I WISH MOM WOULD JUST
GO AHEAD AND DIE SO WE CAN GET ON WITH
EVERYTHING.

OH MY LORD.

I WROTE THAT. I REALLY DID.

ARE YOU HAPPY NOW, SUNNY?

WHAT IS WRONG WITH ME? I SOUND LIKE SUCH
A SPOILED, STUPID LITTLE GIRL.

I THINK I WILL BURN THIS JOURNAL. BURN IT
AND DESTROY MY HORRIBLE THOUGHTS WITH IT.

THOUSANDS OF PEOPLE SURVIVE CANCER. MAYBE
MILLIONS. WHAT ABOUT THAT ARTICLE IN THE PAPER
TODAY ABOUT THE ACTOR WHO SURVIVED -- AND HE'S
NOW TOURING THE COUNTRY WITH A ONE-MAN SHOW
ABOUT HIS LIFE! NOT TO MENTION DAWN'S ARTICLE
ABOUT THE HOLISTIC DOCTOR WHO'S HELPED PEOPLE
GO INTO REMISSION, USING MEDICINE, HERBS, AND
POSITIVE THINKING.

POSITIVE THINKING. THAT'S THE IMPORTANT
THING. IT BUILDS UP ENERGY. KIND OF A FORCE
FIELD OF HEALTHFULNESS. DAWN BELIEVES THAT IS
ABSOLUTELY TRUE.

MOM
WILL
NOT
DIE.
I KNOW IT. I KNOW IT. I KNOW IT.
I HAVE TO GO TO SLEEP.
MY BRAIN IS A MESS.

                    THURSDAY AFTERNOON 10/23
    WRITING THIS ON THE FLY. WELL, ON THE
JOHN, ACTUALLY. NOT ON IT, IN THE USUAL SENSE.
JUST SITTING HERE, WITH THE STALL DOOR SHUT,
TRYING TO HAVE SOME PRIVACY BETWEEN CLASSES.
    SOME DWEEB IS ACTUALLY SMOKING NEAR THE
SINK. IN ORDER TO WRITE DOWN THE NEWS OF THE
DAY WITH A LITTLE PRIVACY, I HAVE TO SIT HERE
AND RISK LUNG CANCER.
    (THIS IS ONE THING I DO NOT LIKE ABOUT
THE SHIFT OF THE EIGHTH GRADE INTO THE HIGH
SCHOOL BUILDING THIS YEAR: A LOT MORE KIDS WHO
SMELL LIKE ASHTRAYS AND THINK THEY'RE WAY COOL.
YUM.)
    OKAY. I HAVE TO SAY THIS:
            MATH BITES!!!

Now I feel better. I have cleared the air.
The smoke doesn't bother me as much.

I was mad at Ms. Whalen today.

First of all, if she weren't such a boring
teacher, maybe I would pay attention in class.
I tried, but I almost fell asleep. So instead,
I read a Newsweek article about cancer
remission rates. It was FILLED with graphs and
numbers and statistics. I was actually learning
a lot of math.

But the Whale had to be sarcastic. When
she saw what I was reading she said something
like, "Since you're smart enough to actually
bypass my lesson plan, perhaps you can share
with us the definition of a tangent."

So I told her, "Just go to any beach.
You'll find tons of them." I mean, it was a
harmless joke. Tan gent. Nobody even got it.

Except for the Whale, who told me I
could practice my "stand-up routine" in the
principal's office.

I was kind of proud of myself. Getting
out of the Whale's class is like escaping
prison.

Not that Mr. Dean's office is exactly fun.
I was kind of expecting him to give me a

BIG ANGRY LECTURE. BUT HE DID SOMETHING WORSE.

He walked in with a tight, closemouthed smile, his eyebrows tenting upward into his creased forehead. I am beginning to recognize this look. The "I feel your pain" look.

"Sunshine," he said in a soft voice (I wonder if he knows how much I <u>hate</u> people calling me by my full name), "if anything's troubling you --"

"I goofed off in Ms. Whalen's class," I explained.

"Yes, I know," Mr. Dean said with a chuckle. "Well, I realize Ms. Whalen can be a bit intense --"

"I was reading a <u>Newsweek</u> article."

"I see. You know, at times of great stress, we all feel the need to escape. But in the long run, we reap the greatest benefit by going on with our lives, sticking to our tasks, trying to give our all. Despite the onset of personal tragedy . . ."

"She's not dead yet, Mr. Dean," I snapped.

Mr. Dean's smile vanished. "I beg your pardon?"

"CAN I GO NOW?"

SOMEHOW I KNEW HE WOULDN'T YELL AT ME. FOR A MOMENT, HIS EYES HAD AN ANGRY GLARE, BUT THEN IT DISAPPEARED. "UH, WELL, SURE, SUNSHINE. IF YOU'RE READY. BUT I JUST WANT YOU TO KNOW, I AM HERE FOR YOU IF YOU NEED TO TALK ABOUT . . . ANYTHING."

"THANKS."

I WAS OUT OF THERE LIKE A SHOT. I WALKED INTO THE FRONT HALLWAY AND LOOKED AT THE SPORTS TROPHY CASE. I WANDERED DOWN TO THE CAFETERIA. I WENT TO THE BATHROOM. AND HERE I AM.

TIME TO GO. DETAILS AT SEVEN.

THURSDAY NIGHT

I WAS WRONG. DETAILS AT 10:44.

IT'S BEEN A LONG NIGHT, AND I AM WIRED. ALSO TOTALLY, TOTALLY CREEPED OUT.

BUT FIRST THINGS FIRST.

OKAY, WHERE WAS I? OH, YES, BACK TO THE JOHN.

I CLOSED MY JOURNAL, WADED THROUGH THE SECONDHAND SMOKE, AND WALKED BACK TO MATH

CLASS -- JUST AS THE PERIOD WAS ENDING.
(PERFECT TIMING!)

THE WHALE, OF COURSE, WAS NOT DONE WITH
ME. AS I PICKED UP MY BOOKS AND LEFT, SHE
CALLED ME OVER TO HER DESK.

"SUNNY," SHE SAID, "YOU'LL BE A LOT HAPPIER
IF YOU STICK TO THE WORK, BELIEVE ME."

THIS WAS SOUNDING FAMILIAR.

"IF YOU JUST PUT YOUR THOUGHTS IN ORDER,"
SHE WENT ON, "MATH CAN BE SIMPLE AND
PREDICTABLE."

YEAH, AND IF I CLICK MY HEELS THREE TIMES,
I'LL GO TO KANSAS. I HATE THE WHALE. I DON'T
KNOW HOW I KEPT MY COOL. BUT I DID. I
THANKED HER AND LEFT.

I DIDN'T SCREAM UNTIL I WAS AROUND THE
CORNER.

UNFORTUNATELY, DUCKY WAS THERE, AND HE
GOT IT FULL BLAST IN THE LEFT EAR.

"YEEOW!" HE SAID.

"PUT YOUR THOUGHTS IN ORDER?" I YELLED.
"THAT'S EASY FOR HER TO SAY! ALL SHE HAS TO
DO IS COME TO SCHOOL AND PUT KIDS TO SLEEP
EVERY DAY. AND SHE GETS PAID FOR IT!"

DUCKY WAS STARING AT ME WITH THIS WEIRD

EXPRESSION. LIKE, <u>WHAT DID I DO TO DESERVE</u>
<u>THIS?</u>

I DON'T BLAME HIM. I MEAN, I BARELY KNOW
HIM. THE FIRST TIME WE MET WAS WHEN HE DROVE
DAWN, MAGGIE, AND ME HOME FROM THAT PARTY --
AND I NEARLY PUKED ALL OVER HIS CAR.

"SUNNY?" HE SAID.

"GROWN-UPS CAN BE SO STUPID," I BARRELED
ON. "DON'T ANY OF THEM REMEMBER WHAT IT WAS
LIKE TO BE A KID?"

"WHOA, WHAT HAPPENED? WHY ARE YOU SO
ANGRY?"

<u>GOT A FEW HOURS?</u> I WANTED TO SAY.

I WAS NOT, HOWEVER, GOING TO MENTION
MOM'S LUMP, WHICH I WASN'T EVEN SUPPOSED TO
KNOW ABOUT. NOT IN THE MIDDLE OF THE HALLWAY
OF VISTA TO A GUY I HARDLY EVEN KNEW.

THEN I LOOKED UP AT DUCKY.

HE WAS GIVING ME THIS CONCERNED LOOK. BUT
FRIENDLY CONCERNED, NOT PHONY LIKE MR. DEAN.

"I MEAN, HEY, YOU DON'T HAVE TO TELL ME,"
HE SAID WITH A SMILE. "I'LL WALK YOU TO YOUR
LOCKER?"

I DON'T KNOW WHY, BUT I JUST CALMED
RIGHT DOWN. SOMETHING ABOUT THAT EXPRESSION.

OR MAYBE IT'S JUST HIS FACE IN GENERAL. IT'S SO OPEN.

Ducky HAS GREAT EYES. REALLY LARGE AND DARK AND BEAUTIFUL. WHICH, I GUESS, IS WHY SOME OF THE OLDER GUYS CALL HIM BAMBI. WHEN THEY'RE NOT QUACKING AT HIM OR MAKING FUN OF HIS CLOTHES.

I DON'T KNOW HOW HE PUTS UP WITH THOSE JERKS. GUYS ARE SO WEIRD. IT'S LIKE, WHEN THEY REACH A CERTAIN AGE, THEY HAVE TO DROP THEIR SENSE OF HUMOR AND FORGET ABOUT STYLE. TODAY, FOR INSTANCE. 90 PERCENT OF THE GUYS SHOWED UP IN T-SHIRTS WITH FLANNEL SHIRTS OVER THEM. IT'S LIKE, THE UNIFORM. DUCKY? A BOWLING SHIRT, COOL SNEAKERS, AND GREEN OVERDYED JEANS. MORE GUYS SHOULD DO THAT.

AND MORE SHOULD LEARN HOW TO LISTEN, LIKE DUCKY WAS DOING.

"JUST . . . STRESSED OUT, I GUESS," I REPLIED. "I DIDN'T SLEEP TOO GREAT LAST NIGHT."

DUCKY NODDED, AND WE BOTH STARTED HEADING TOWARD THE LOCKERS. "YOU KNOW WHAT I DO?" HE SAID. "FORCE MY EYES OPEN. THAT WAY, YOU'RE NOT FIGHTING YOUR BODY. YOU'RE FAKING IT OUT. IT WANTS TO STAY AWAKE? FINE. STARE AT A POINT ON YOUR CEILING. JUST STARE. IN FIVE

OR TEN MINUTES, GUARANTEED, YOUR EYES ARE CLOSING LIKE IRON DOORS."

WE TURNED THE CORNER NEAR OUR SECTION OF LOCKERS. DAWN AND MAGGIE WERE ALREADY THERE, GABBING AWAY.

MAGGIE WAS LOOKING VERY FUTURE-VETERINARIAN-OF-AMERICA. DAWN, OF COURSE, LOOKED LIKE . . . DAWN -- A PEASANT BLOUSE AND JEANS, DOC MARTENS. HER LONG BLONDE HAIR WAS GATHERED AT THE TOP IN A FRENCH BRAID.

"YOU HAVE LOCKERS TOGETHER?" DUCKY ASKED WITH A GRIN. "SO I CAN, LIKE, BOTHER YOU ALL AT ONCE?"

"OH, HI, DUCKY," MAGGIE SAID AS IF SHE'D KNOWN HIM FOR YEARS. "I GUESS I CAN INVITE YOU OVER TONIGHT TOO."

"INVITE?" DUCKY AND I BOTH ASKED AT THE SAME TIME AS I HEADED FOR MY LOCKER.

"DAD HAS A ROUGH VIDEO EDIT OF FATAL JUDGMENT," MAGGIE EXPLAINED, "THIS UPCOMING THRILLER? HE BROUGHT HOME FROM THE STUDIO? WE HAVE TO PROMISE NOT TO TALK ABOUT IT, THOUGH -- OTHERWISE WE COULD GET SUED OR SOMETHING."

"COOL," DUCKY SAID.

I MUST HAVE BEEN IN A FOG. I WAS NOT

REALLY LISTENING TO THE CONVERSATION. I WAS
THINKING ABOUT THE WHALE'S CLASS AND MY VISIT
TO MR. DEAN'S OFFICE -- AND I WAS REALLY GLAD
THE DAY WAS OVER.

DAWN WALKED HOME WITH ME. ON THE WAY, I
TOLD HER WHAT HAD HAPPENED WITH THE WHALE.

"YOU DIDN'T!" SHE CRIED OUT. "SUNNY, YOU'RE
ALL WOUND UP. YOU NEED A VACATION IN SOME
FARAWAY PLACE."

"VENUS MIGHT BE NICE."

"HAVE YOU TRIED MEDITATING?"

I MEAN, REALLY. I JUST BURST OUT
LAUGHING. DAWN DIDN'T LOOK TOO PLEASED.

"I'M SERIOUS," SHE SAID. "I'VE TRIED IT. IT
STOPS ALL YOUR BAD THOUGHTS. YOU KNOW,
SOMETIMES IT'S NOT EASY HAVING A STEPMOTHER
LIKE CAROL --"

AT LEAST CAROL IS HEALTHY, I DIDN'T SAY.

MOM AND DAD'S OLD PHOTO ALBUMS POPPED
INTO MY MIND. THE HIPPIE PICTURES. THE OLD,
PAINTED VOLKSWAGENS, THE FRINGED BELL-BOTTOMS,
THE PEACE SIGNS, THE SUMMER IN THE BUDDHIST
RETREAT -- EVERYTHING SEEMS SO QUAINT AND CUTE.
MOM MUST HAVE WEIGHED ABOUT 90 POUNDS.
(ACTUALLY, SHE'S PROBABLY CLOSE TO THAT NOW,
BUT SHE LOOKS MUCH DIFFERENT.) AND DAD, WITH

HIS LONG, KINKY HAIR PAST HIS SHOULDERS, AND A CHESTFUL OF BEADS. WHAT WAS THEIR FAVORITE PASTIME BACK THEN? MEDITATION.

"THAT'S SOMETHING MY PARENTS USED TO DO," I SAID. "IT DIDN'T HELP THEM."

"HOW DO YOU KNOW?" DAWN REPLIED. "YOUR PARENTS ARE TWO OF THE NICEST, MOST CENTERED PEOPLE I KNOW."

"YEAH, CENTERED ON THEMSELVES," I MUTTERED.

"WHAT?"

"NOTHING."

THAT WAS NASTY.

BUT IT FELT GOOD TO SAY IT.

LATER THURSDAY NIGHT

I THOUGHT I WAS SLEEPY.

WRONG AGAIN.

JUST AS WELL. I NEVER DID FINISH WRITING ABOUT TONIGHT, AND I HAVE TO. I STILL FEEL SO WEIRD ABOUT WHAT HAPPENED.

OKAY. BACK TO WHERE I LEFT OFF. MEDITATION. I WAS TRYING TO TAKE DAWN'S ADVICE SERIOUSLY AS I WALKED INSIDE THE HOUSE.

My thoughts were so sour, my brain was about to curdle.

As I reached into the mailbox, I pretended my mind was a big blackboard. On it were all the images of the day -- Ms. Whalen, Mr. Dean, the smoke in the bathroom. I took a big mental eraser and began wiping from right to left.

STOP . . . ALL . . . THOUGHTS.

I started feeling blank. Empty.

Not exactly exciting, but better than being depressed.

As I opened the front door, I glanced at the mail.

A hospital bill, with the word URGENT stamped on the front. (BING! I thought of Mom, lying on the hospital bed.)

A big envelope from Dad's HMO. (I imagined Dad arguing over the phone about insurance.)

A catalog from Alfredo Puccini Wigs and Hair Design. (I pictured Mom trying on an ugly wig like the one on the cover.)

A letter from a wills and estates lawyer. (I don't even want to mention what THAT brought to mind.)

MEDITATION? RIGHT. NOT IN THIS LIFETIME.

I STEPPED INTO THE FRONT HALLWAY AND DROPPED THE MAIL ON THE END TABLE, RIGHT NEXT TO THE ANSWERING MACHINE.

IT WAS BLINKING "1," SO I PRESSED THE PLAYBACK BUTTON.

"SUNNY?" DAD'S VOICE SAID URGENTLY. "CALL ME AT WORK, AS SOON AS YOU GET IN."

CLICK.

THAT WAS IT. NO GOOD-BYE, NO NOTHING.

SOMETHING WAS WRONG. SOMETHING HE COULDN'T TALK ABOUT.

MY HEART WAS RACING. I PICKED UP THE RECEIVER AND PRESSED THE AUTODIAL BUTTON FOR THE BOOKSTORE.

"WINSLOW BOOKS," DAD'S VOICE SAID.

"IS MOM ALL RIGHT?" THE WORDS FLEW OUT OF MY MOUTH.

"HI, SUNNY! CAN YOU HOLD A MOMENT?"

CLICK.

JUST LIKE THAT. I'M PRACTICALLY PASSING OUT, AND HE PUTS ME ON HOLD. I NEARLY SCREAMED.

CLICK. "SORRY, SUNNY, IT'S CRAZY HERE. THE GOOD NEWS IS, MOM'S COMING HOME TOMORROW. AT SIX P.M."

"You mean . . . the lump . . . ?"

Ugh. I wanted to swallow the words right back down. Dad had never told me about the lump. Now he knew I'd been eavesdropping.

"Benign, thank goodness," Dad replied, "and easily treated. Not to worry. Now the bad news."

I braced myself.

"The fridge is empty," Dad went on, "and I'm going to be stuck here until at least eleven. So could you pick up a few groceries at Leo's? You know, stuff Mom can eat when she arrives home. Tell Leo to bill it, okay?"

"Sure," I muttered. "'Bye."

I hung up the phone and slumped against the wall.

I was sweating. My heartbeat was going like a tom-tom. As I let the news sink in, I began calming down.

Mom was going to be all right. For now.

Then I began to be mad at Dad. He couldn't have left a more detailed message on the machine so I wouldn't worry? He had to turn me into a stress case -- over what? A piece of good news and a shopping list?

And why hadn't he cared that I'd

EAVESDROPPED? THAT BOTHERED ME. WASN'T I IMPORTANT ENOUGH TO BE ANGRY AT?

IN THAT FABULOUS MOOD, I WENT ON MY SHOPPING TRIP.

OF COURSE, I _HAD_ TO BUY TOO MUCH TO FIT IN MY BACKPACK. LEO SCOWLED AT ME WHEN I RETURNED SOME OF IT. (I DON'T KNOW WHY HE WAS SO ANGRY. _I_ WAS THE ONE WHO HAD TO LUG IT HOME ON A BIKE.)

I WAS STARVING WHEN I ARRIVED. I HELPED MYSELF TO A DINNER OF BRUISED FRUITS AND VEGETABLES.

I'D BARELY STARTED EATING WHEN THE BLEEPING OF THE PHONE NEARLY MADE ME JUMP OUT OF MY SKIN. I CANNOT GET USED TO DAD'S HABIT OF TURNING THE KITCHEN PHONE RINGER ON HIGH WHENEVER MOM IS IN THE HOSPITAL.

I GRABBED THE RECEIVER. "HELLO?"

"HI, SUNNY!" MOM SAID. "UM, I GUESS YOU COULDN'T MAKE IT?"

OH MY GOD.

I'D PROMISED MOM I WOULD VISIT. AND THEN WHAT DID I DO? TOTALLY FORGET.

DUH.

WHAT A FOOL.

I APOLOGIZED ABOUT A THOUSAND TIMES. I

COULD TELL MOM WAS HURT, BUT SHE KEPT ON INSISTING IT WAS OKAY. "I'LL BE COMING HOME TOMORROW, AFTER ALL," SHE REMINDED ME.

"I'LL HELP BRING YOU BACK," I INSISTED.

"GREAT," MOM REPLIED. "YOU'LL MEET MY SUPPORT GROUP." SHE WENT ON ABOUT THEM FOR AWHILE, ABOUT HOW THEY'D ALL SURVIVED CANCER AND GONE ON TO LEAD NORMAL LIVES. THAT WAS ENCOURAGING, I GUESS.

THEN, JUST AS MOM WAS GOING TO HANG UP, SHE LET GO OF THE BIG ONE. "OH! I ALMOST FORGOT. HOW DID YOU LIKE THE LITTLE SURPRISE ON YOUR DRESSER?"

"UH, WHAT SURPRISE?"

"I ASKED YOUR DAD TO LEAVE IT THERE TODAY. I MEANT TO GIVE IT TO YOU BEFORE I LEFT --"

"I HAVEN'T BEEN UPSTAIRS YET. HANG ON. I'LL CHECK."

I RAN UP TO MY ROOM. SITTING IN THE MIDDLE OF MY DRESSER WAS AN ANCIENT GIFT BOX.

I TOOK OFF THE TOP AND PULLED OUT ANOTHER BOX. THIS ONE HAD A HINGED TOP AND WAS MADE OF DARK WOOD, WITH MUSIC NOTES CARVED INTO THE SIDES. I OPENED IT AND A LULLABY BEGAN TINKLING. I KIND OF RECOGNIZED

IT, BUT IT SOUNDED AS IF SOME OF THE NOTES
WERE MISSING. INSIDE THE BOX, A TINY PORCELAIN
BALLERINA TWIRLED JERKILY. HER TUTU WAS
YELLOWED WITH AGE, AND SOME OF HER FACIAL
FEATURES WERE MISSING.

MY FIRST THOUGHT WAS: MOM IS LOSING IT. I
MEAN, I MIGHT HAVE ENJOYED THIS WHEN I WAS
FOUR OR FIVE.

MY SECOND THOUGHT WAS: DAD MADE A
MISTAKE AND PUT THE WRONG THING ON MY
DRESSER.

I WENT INTO MOM AND DAD'S ROOM AND
PICKED UP THE PHONE EXTENSION. "A MUSIC BOX?"
I SAID.

"I KNOW, IT'S CORNY --"

"NO! IT'S JUST THAT -- WELL, I'M JUST NOT
SURE WHY YOU GAVE IT TO ME."

"IT'S AN HEIRLOOM," MOM EXPLAINED. "MY
GRANDMA LEFT IT TO ME. IT MAY BE VALUABLE. I
FIGURED YOU SHOULD HAVE IT."

"MO-OM, THAT'S THE KIND OF THING YOU DO
WHEN YOU'RE ABOUT TO --" I ALMOST SAID DIE.
BUT I STOPPED MYSELF. "WHEN YOU'RE ABOUT TO
HAVE GRANDCHILDREN OR SOMETHING."

MOM LAUGHED. "OH, WELL. SAVE IT FOR
THEM."

WE TALKED AWHILE LONGER, THEN SAID GOOD
NIGHT.

I WALKED BACK TO MY ROOM AND SET THE
MUSIC BOX ON MY DRESSER.

AN HEIRLOOM. THE WORD WAS SPINNING
AROUND IN MY HEAD. IT STILL IS. HOW CAN MOM
BE THINKING OF HEIRLOOMS?

STOP . . . ALL . . . THOUGHTS.

IT DOESN'T WORK. WRITING THE WORDS DOWN
DOESN'T EVEN HELP.

AFTER THE PHONE CALL, I WALKED DOWNSTAIRS.
MY APPETITE WAS PRACTICALLY GONE. I NIBBLED
ON SOME CARROTS AND MADE A SMALL SALAD, BUT
THAT WAS ABOUT IT.

I READ A LITTLE, WATCHED A LITTLE TV, AND
WENT TO BED EARLY. AND NOW HERE I AM, STILL
WIDE AWAKE.

THE LIGHT IS CASTING WEIRD SHADOWS. ON MY
DRESSER, THE MUSIC BOX LOOKS ABOUT THREE FEET
TALL.

THERE. I JUST PUT IT IN THE CLOSET, BEHIND
MY SHOE BOXES ON THE TOP SHELF. I FEEL
BETTER NOW.

THE TROUBLE IS, I'M STILL WIDE AWAKE.

MAYBE I'LL TAKE DUCKY'S ADVICE.

JUST KEEP MY EYES OPEN AND STARE AT THE CEILING.

FRIDAY 10/24
10:00 A.M.

IT WORKED. AFTER ABOUT TWO HOURS OF STARING.

I AM FED UP.

I AM WASHED OUT.

I CANNOT FACE ANOTHER DAY OF TRYING TO STAY AWAKE AT SCHOOL.

SO I WON'T. I AM GOING TO DO SOMETHING FOR ME. SOMETHING I DESERVE.

I AM ABOUT TO TAKE MYSELF ON A TRIP.

IT ALL STARTED THIS MORNING, WHEN I COULDN'T GET OUT OF BED. I SMELLED THE COFFEE DAD WAS MAKING DOWNSTAIRS, I HEARD HIM CALL OUT MY NAME, I HEARD THE RADIO BLASTING.

BUT. I. COULD. NOT. MOVE.

I FINALLY WOKE UP WHEN I HEARD DAWN'S VOICE OUTSIDE MY WINDOW, SAYING GOOD-BYE TO HER PARENTS AS SHE WAS LEAVING FOR SCHOOL.

School.

Hackett. Whalen. Dean.

The idea made me sick.

I stumbled to my closet and opened the door.

What a pathetic sight. It looked like a rack at the thrift shop after a busy day.

I realized no one had done laundry in ages.

Duh. Had I expected the clothes to clean themselves? Dad was too busy, Mom was in the hospital. I should have thought of it myself.

I went to the bathroom hamper and grabbed an armful of clothes. I staggered downstairs, threw them in the washing machine, and turned it to the quickest setting.

To get to school by 8:40, I'd have to fly.

As I fixed myself breakfast, I flipped on the radio and heard the weather report.

Bright. Temperatures near 90. Good air quality. The last thing the announcer said was, "The surf's up, dudes!"

That was when I had my idea.

A VACATION.

NO BIG DEAL. JUST A HALF DAY AWAY FROM SCHOOL, AWAY FROM DAD AND ALL THE STRESS.

THE SUN WOULD FEEL GREAT. THE WATER WOULD BE NICE AND WARM. I WOULD BE ALONE!

AND I WOULDN'T HAVE TO WAIT FOR THE LAUNDRY. ALL MY BATHING SUITS WERE CLEAN.

I HAD TO DO IT. HAD TO.

OKAY, I'D MISS SOME CLASSES. BUT BIG DEAL. IN HOMEROOM, MR. LEAVITT NEVER DOES ANYTHING EXCEPT READ THE NEWSPAPER ALOUD ANYWAY. AND MS. CARTER'S AT SOME CONFERENCE, SO THERE WOULD BE A SUB FOR FIRST PERIOD. AND THEN STUDY HALL, FOLLOWED BY GYM . . .

NO ONE WOULD EVEN NOTICE I WAS GONE. THIS WAS GREAT.

HOW FAR WAS THE BEACH BY BUS? IT COULDN'T BE TOO FAR. AMY AND BARRY CLAY TAKE THE TRIP ALL THE TIME TO VISIT THEIR DAD AT HIS CONCESSION STAND THERE.

AND I KNEW FOR A FACT THAT THE BUSES RUN ALL DAY.

I RAN UPSTAIRS AND CHANGED INTO A BATHING SUIT. I MANAGED TO FIND AN OLD DISNEYLAND T-SHIRT AND A PAIR OF RIPPED shorts. I put them on over the suit, loaded all my money into my pocket, and headed back downstairs.

The washer was still going. No problem. I'd finish up after school.

I took my backpack, grabbed a towel from the bathroom, and got ready to leave.

Now I am at the bus shelter, sitting on the bench. I'm feeling a little weird about this. I keep thinking some big van with truant officers will squeal around the corner to pick me up.

Do truant officers exist anymore? I doubt it.

Well, just in case, I'm wearing my big, floppy hat and sunglasses. Frankly, I think I look pretty cool. I can always pretend I'm someone else. Call myself Angelica or Camilla or something.

Palo what? Sunny who?

For today, that world and that person don't exist.

I am free.

AM ON THE BUS NOW. HAVE DECIDED NOT TO GO TO PALO CITY BEACH.

I REALIZED MR. CLAY WILL BE THERE. EVEN IF I STAY AWAY FROM HIS CONCESSION STAND, HE MIGHT SEE ME. AND HE MIGHT RECOGNIZE ME. EVEN WITH MY DISGUISE.

SECOND, WHAT IF ONE OF MY SURFER BUDDIES SEES ME? WHAT IF MS. CARTER REALLY DIDN'T HAVE TO GO TO A CONFERENCE, AND SHE'S OUT SOAKING UP RAYS?

IT'S JUST TOO BIG OF A RISK.

SO I'VE DECIDED TO STAY ON THE BUS UNTIL THE END OF THE LINE: VENICE BEACH.

I CAN'T REMEMBER HOW FAR THAT IS. I KNOW IT'S NEAR L.A., AROUND THE SANTA MONICA AREA.

ON THE PLUS SIDE, I'M SURE NO ONE THERE WILL RECOGNIZE ME. ON THE MINUS SIDE, IT MAY TAKE FOREVER TO GET THERE.

OH, WELL, IF IT DOES, I'LL JUST STAY ON THE BUS AND COME BACK. NO BIG DEAL.

I HAVE BEEN HERE ABOUT A HALF HOUR. JUST WALKING.

IT'S WEIRD TO BE HERE IN THE MIDDLE OF A SCHOOL DAY. NOT ONE FAMILIAR FACE. NO ONE CALLING TO ME. NO ONE TELLING ME WHERE TO GO OR WHAT TO DO.

I AM SCARED OUT OF MY MIND.

I AM HAVING THE TIME OF MY LIFE.

VENICE BEACH IS SO PEACEFUL. THE SURF'S CALM, SO THE WATER IS DOTTED WITH BATHERS LYING ON THEIR BOARDS, WAITING. TO MY RIGHT, A FEW PEOPLE ARE TRYING TO FLY KITES. TO MY LEFT, SOME WEIGHT LIFTERS ARE WORKING OUT IN AN OUTDOOR, PENNED-IN AREA ON THE SAND. MOST OF THEM ARE GUYS. I CAN'T STOP STARING AT THEIR BODS. THEIR NECKS ARE THE SIZE OF TREE TRUNKS. THEIR PECS LOOK AS IF THEY'RE CARVED OUT OF STONE.

A LITTLE WAY DOWN THE BOARDWALK, SOMEONE HAS SET UP A BOOM BOX. BLADERS ARE WHIZZING BY AT BLINDING SPEED, TURNING, DANCING,

LEAPING. I CAN'T BELIEVE SOME OF THE BATHING SUITS. THEY SHOW PRACTICALLY EVERYTHING.

I'M SITTING NEXT TO THIS PLACE THAT SELLS FRESH-SQUEEZED FRUIT JUICES. IT SMELLS GREAT. I THINK I'LL HAVE A "KIWI-PINEAPPLE-STRAWBERRY-HONEYDEW HI-ENERGY ZINGER" AND LAY IN THE SUN.

WHAT A LIFE.

I COULD MAKE A HABIT OF THIS.

FRIDAY
1:17 P.M.

I STAYED WAY TOO LONG. THE BUS IS COMING IN THREE MINUTES. IF IT'S ON TIME, I CAN MAKE LAST PERIOD. MAYBE.

AT LEAST I'LL BE HOME AROUND THE TIME I ALWAYS RETURN FROM SCHOOL, IN CASE DAD CALLS. WHICH HE PROBABLY WON'T.

STILL, I HAVE TO GO. OR I MAY STAY HERE FOREVER.

MY LIFE HAS BEEN CHANGED, BIG-TIME.

I WAS HAVING A GOOD ENOUGH DAY JUST HANGING OUT. I SWAM, I SNACKED, I EVEN HAD A LONG CONVERSATION WITH A CUTE SURFER.

THAT WOULD HAVE BEEN FINE. I WAS ALL SET
TO LEAVE VENICE BEACH AT 11:00, AND I WOULD
HAVE BOARDED THAT BUS WITH A BIG, SATISFIED
SMILE ON MY FACE.

I ALMOST DID, TOO.

BUT THEN I MET HIM.

AND NOW I'M FLOATING.

I WAS SITTING ON A BENCH, BRUSHING OFF MY
FEET SO I COULD PUT ON MY SANDALS. I COULD
SEE (AND FEEL) A SPLINTER JUST UNDER THE BIG
TOE OF MY RIGHT FOOT. SO I CROSSED MY LEGS,
TURNED MY FOOT SOLE-UP, AND TRIED TO SQUEEZE
THE SPLINTER OUT.

THERE I SAT, IN THAT ATTRACTIVE AND
FLATTERING POSITION, MY FACE INCHES AWAY FROM
MY THROBBING TOE, WHEN A GUY PLOPPED ONTO
THE BENCH NEXT TO ME.

I GLANCED UP AND NEARLY FELL OVER.

HE WAS CUTE, BUT NOT IN A MODEL-Y WAY.
TOUGHER. STRONG, CHISELED-LOOKING CHIN, SLIGHTLY
CROOKED NOSE THAT LOOKED AS IF IT HAD BEEN
BROKEN. HE HAD A GREAT TAN TOO. I FIGURED
HE WAS EIGHTEEN OR SO.

HIS SHIRT WAS OFF, WRAPPED AROUND HIS
WAIST, AND A GREEN BACKPACK LAY ON THE

GROUND NEAR HIS LEGS. As HE LEANED OVER TO ADJUST HIS BLADES, HIS WAVY BLACK HAIR FELL OVER HIS FACE.

WHICH WAS TOO BAD. SORT OF LIKE DRAWING A CURTAIN OVER A WORK OF ART.

I LET MY FOOT DROP TO THE BOARDWALK.

"SPLINTER?" HE ASKED.

GREAT. HE'D SEEN ME COMMUNING WITH MY TOES.

"UH . . . HUH-HUH-HUH," I BEGAN. WHAT WAS I DOING? AGREEING? LAUGHING? TRYING TO SAY AN ACTUAL WORD? I HAVE NO IDEA. THAT'S JUST WHAT CAME OUT.

"YOU'RE BETTER OFF SITTING ON THE JETTY," HE SAID.

DUH, ANSWERED MY FACE. AT THIS POINT, I HAVE NO IDEA WHY HE WASN'T BLADING AWAY FULL SPEED.

HE NODDED TOWARD THE SURF. "SIT ON THE ROCKS AND DIP YOUR FOOT IN THE SALT WATER. THAT'LL WASH OFF THE SAND AND SOFTEN THE SKIN. A COUPLE OF SCRATCHES, AND THAT BABY IS OUT OF THERE."

"OH." I WAS MANAGING SOME FULLY FORMED WORDS NOW. "OKAY."

Now he was looking straight at me -- and smiling. Smiling! Why? I hadn't even given him a hint that I spoke English.

But I didn't mind it a bit.

Some writer once said that the eyes are the windows to the soul. I believe it. Anyone who looked into Dawn's eyes would see her optimism and strength. Catch Ducky's glance for a second and you think: compassion, sense of humor.

I was looking through the clearest blue-green window now. The soul inside was speaking loudly. I didn't understand the words, but I liked the message. I liked it a lot.

"You ever been out there?" he asked. He was taking off his blades now.

"Where, the jetty? Sure," I lied.

"I haven't. I don't live around here." He tied his blades together, put them in his pack, then stood up and slung the pack over his shoulder. "Come on."

He was crossing the boardwalk now, heading toward the beach in the direction of the jetty.

I glanced over at the bus stop. A bus was pulling away.

PANIC.

I SHOOK MYSELF. I GAVE MYSELF A GOOD, QUICK, MENTAL SLAP IN THE FACE.

FORGET ABOUT THE BUS. TIME TO GROW UP. TIME TO SEIZE THE MOMENT AND BE MYSELF.

I QUICKLY CAUGHT UP TO THE GUY.

OKAY, NOW, I WILL _TRY_ TO REMEMBER OUR WHOLE CONVERSATION. I THINK I CAN. MY MIND SORT OF TAPE-RECORDED IT.

"WHERE ARE YOU FROM?" I ASKED.

"ALL OVER. I WAS IN SAN DIEGO FOR AWHILE. LAS VEGAS BEFORE THAT." HE SMILED. "I COULD TAKE ONLY ABOUT TWO DAYS OF THAT."

I LAUGHED. "OH, YEAH. I KNOW WHAT YOU MEAN." (GACK. HAVE I EVER BEEN TO VEGAS? DO ALLIGATORS FLY?)

"WHAT'S YOUR NAME?" HE ASKED.

"CAMILLA." I DO NOT KNOW WHY I SAID THAT. I COULD FEEL MY INSIDES FLINCH. MUST HAVE BEEN MY SOUL TALKING. "YOU?"

"CARSON."

"CARSON WHAT?"

"JUST CARSON." HE DUG INTO HIS POCKET AND PULLED OUT A HALF-EATEN BAG OF NUTS. HE THREW A FEW TOWARD AN EMPTY SECTION OF BEACH.

A flock of seagulls swooped down out of nowhere. Some of them grabbed the little morsels and flew off, while the others screeched angrily.

Carson laughed. "When I was in Texas, some guy hired me to work at the airport. The job was to shoot seagulls, to keep them from getting sucked into jet engines."

"Ewww, are you joking?" I said. "You did that?"

"No way. Soon as I heard the job description, I was out of there. I worked in a bookstore instead."

"Really? My dad owns a bookstore."

"It's boring, but you get to read. I wanted to work in the music section, but I was the youngest one there, and everybody thought they could boss me around. So I quit."

"So, how old are you?"

"Closer to birth than death, I hope."

"Big help!"

We were at the jetty now. Carson picked up a flat rock and skimmed it on the surface of the water. "Age is a bad traveling companion."

I THINK THAT WAS WHAT HE SAID. SOMETHING LIKE THAT.

WE BOTH WALKED ONTO THE JETTY ROCKS. THE TIDE WAS HIGH, SO WHEN WE SAT DOWN, OUR FEET DANGLED IN THE WATER.

"So YOU JUST . . . WANDER AROUND," I SAID.

CARSON NODDED. "YUP. NO TIES, NO LIES. I STAY WHERE I LIKE, I LEAVE WHEN I'M READY. I WORK WHEN I NEED TO AND LIVE SIMPLE. I LIKE IT THAT WAY. WHEN YOU'RE TIED DOWN, YOU'RE ALWAYS MAKING COMPROMISES, YOU KNOW? I LIKE BEING TOTALLY FREE."

WHOA. TALK ABOUT TWO SOULS MATCHING. HE WAS TAKING THE WORDS RIGHT OUT OF MY MIND. I LIKED HIS PHILOSOPHY A LOT. "I FEEL THE SAME WAY," I SAID.

"MOST PEOPLE DON'T, EVEN WHEN THEY SAY THEY DO," CARSON WENT ON. "I GUESS I'M JUST A FREE SPIRIT."

"ME TOO."

"ARE YOU INTO KEROUAC?"

"WHAT?"

"JACK KEROUAC? ON THE ROAD?" HE PULLED A RAGGEDY PAPERBACK OUT OF HIS PACK.

"OH, THAT. UH, WELL, SORT OF, BUT NOT

LATELY. I MEAN, I HAVEN'T LOOKED AT IT IN A LONG TIME." (LIKE MY WHOLE LIFE.)

"YOU SHOULD READ IT. THAT AND <u>CATCHER IN THE RYE</u>. THOSE GUYS ARE ME. TOTALLY." I THOUGHT HE WAS GOING TO LEND ME THE BOOK, BUT HE PUT IT INTO HIS PACK AGAIN. "HOW'S THE SPLINTER?"

I RAISED MY FOOT OUT OF THE WATER. I WAS ABOUT TO LIFT IT TO LOOK AT MY TOE, WHEN CARSON REACHED DOWN AND TOOK MY FOOT IN HIS HAND.

"SIT BACK," HE SAID.

IT WASN'T EASY FINDING A COMFORTABLE POSITION, BUT I DID. THE SUN WAS BRIGHT, SO I SHIELDED MY EYES WITH MY ARM.

I COULDN'T SEE WHAT EXACTLY CARSON WAS DOING. I FELT A SHORT, SHARP PAIN. JUST A TWINGE.

"THERE," HE SAID. "DONE."

I SAT FORWARD AGAIN. I LOOKED AT THE BOTTOM OF MY TOE AS GRACEFULLY AS I COULD MANAGE.

THE SPLINTER WAS GONE. ONLY A FAINT, STRAIGHT PINK LINE REMAINED.

"THANKS," I SAID.

"No problem." Carson grinned and stood up. "Well, see you."

"Wait! I mean, you're going?"

"New blades. I need to break them in."

"Oh, right."

Carson began walking back toward the boardwalk.

"You know, I have some too," I blurted out, limping after him. "Blades, I mean. At home, though."

"Cool," Carson replied. "You should bring them here."

"I will. Maybe we can blade together."

"Whatever," Carson said with a shrug.

But it was a friendly shrug. And a positive kind of whatever. Although you can't always tell.

We didn't say much more. My foot kind of ached, and he walked fast, so I had to concentrate just to keep up.

He was already sitting on a bench, putting on his blades, when I reached him.

A moment later he was on his feet, picking up his backpack. "Watch those splinters," he said with a smile.

AND THAT WAS IT. HE WAS OFF, ROCKING
FROM SIDE TO SIDE AS HE GLIDED INTO THE CROWD.

BUT HIS SMILE IS STILL WITH ME. I CANNOT
WIPE IT FROM MY BRAIN.

IT STAYED THERE WHILE I PUT ON MY
SANDALS. IT STAYED THERE WHILE I LOOKED AT
THE BUS SCHEDULE.

AND IT'S STILL HERE, LOOKING OVER MY
SHOULDER, FLOATING IN THE AIR LIKE THE GRIN OF
THE CHESHIRE CAT, ONLY BETTER.

STAYED TUNED FOR PART TWO.

SOMEDAY.

YUCK. SORRY. THAT STAIN UNDER THE LAST
ENTRY IS KUNG PAO SAUCE. OKAY, I'M A TOTAL
PIG. BUT I'M STARVING, AND I'M BEING FORCED
TO EAT TAKEOUT CHINESE FOOD IN MY ROOM,
ALONE.

WELL, NOT FORCED. I CHOSE TO COME HERE.
IT BEATS SITTING IN A LIVING ROOM FULL OF
STRANGE GROWN-UPS ASKING ME DUMB QUESTIONS

WHILE I'M TRYING TO EAT TOFU WITH KUNG PAO
SAUCE.

I COULD HAVE PICKED UP SOME LUNCH AT
VENICE BEACH, BUT DID I? NOOOOO. OF ALL DAYS
TO FORGET. THE BEACH WORE ME OUT. IT'S NOT
LIKE I <u>DID</u> ANYTHING EXCEPT MEET MY MATCH, THE
ABSOLUTE COOLEST GUY ON THE WEST COAST --

<u>YOU ARE EXAGGERATING, SUNNY. YOU DON'T
KNOW A THING ABOUT HIM. HE IS STILL A
STRANGER. YOU MAY NEVER SEE HIM AGAIN. GET
OVER IT.</u>

OKAY, NOW THAT I'VE GOTTEN THAT OUT OF
THE WAY, I CAN LET MY INNER SELF SPEAK.

I WANT TO SEE HIM AGAIN.

CARSON. IT'S <u>SUCH</u> A COOL NAME. I WONDER
WHAT IT MEANS. PROBABLY SOMETHING LIKE "NOBLE
WARRIOR" IN WELSH. OR MAYBE SOMETHING MORE
HUMBLE, LIKE "EXCELLENT SPLINTER REMOVER."

THE BAD THING ABOUT A NAME LIKE SUNSHINE
IS THAT IT HAS NO MYSTERY.

ANYWAY, I DIDN'T FINISH WRITING ABOUT MY
TRIP, SO HERE GOES.

HOW COULD I GO TO SCHOOL AFTER THAT? IT
JUST DIDN'T MAKE SENSE TO SHOW UP RIGHT
BEFORE THE FINAL BELL. BESIDES, IT'S EASIER TO

MAKE UP AN EXCUSE FOR MISSING A WHOLE DAY
THAN PART OF ONE.

I WAS DEEPLY MOURNING THE LOSS OF
CARSON. BUT I WAS ALSO REENTERING MY REAL
LIFE, AND THAT FACT WAS MAKING MY STOMACH
RUMBLE.

As I WALKED UP ELDORA ROAD, I WAS
BEGINNING TO REALIZE THAT GOING TO THE BEACH
WAS A MAJOR STUPID MISTAKE.

WHAT IF DAD HAD COME HOME? WHAT IF MR.
DEAN'S OFFICE HAD LEFT A MESSAGE ON OUR
ANSWERING MACHINE, ASKING WHERE I WAS? WHAT
IF DAWN OR MAGGIE HAD CALLED?

OR ALL OF THEM?

WHAT IF SOMETHING HAD HAPPENED TO MOM
AND I WAS MILES AWAY, PLAYING HOOKY AND
TALKING TO TOTAL STRANGERS?

WHO DID I THINK I WAS, ANYWAY, MESSING UP
SO MANY PEOPLE'S LIVES FOR A DAY AT THE
BEACH?

I THOUGHT THAT UNTIL I WALKED INSIDE THE
HOUSE. THEN I GOT OVER IT.

DAD WASN'T HOME. THE ANSWERING MACHINE
WAS FLASHING A BIG ZERO. NOTHING HAD HAPPENED.

WHICH IS EXACTLY WHAT I'D PREDICTED.

I STILL HAD PLENTY OF TIME TO HELP BRING

Mom home from the hospital. She was supposed to be released at six.

Dumping my backpack, I ran outside and fetched my bike from the garage.

As I sped down the driveway, I almost ran into Dawn.

"Is everything okay?" was her greeting. "When you didn't show up for dinner at Maggie's last night, we were all worried that something had happened -- you know, with your mom."

Ugh. I had totally forgotten Maggie's dinner invitation.

I hate having to apologize all the time. But I did, again.

When Dawn started prying about where I'd been today, I just cut her off. I told her I had to go pick up Mom.

It was the truth.

I figure I'll tell her the rest when I have some more time.

Like next year.

Mom was in a great mood when I walked in. She was dressed in her regular clothes and sitting up at the edge of her bed. She gave me a big hug and kiss.

I WAS SO RELIEVED — ONE, THAT NOTHING BAD HAD HAPPENED TO HER WHILE I'D BEEN GONE, AND TWO, THAT SHE HAD NO IDEA I'D CUT SCHOOL.

"WHAT CAN I DO TO HELP?" I ASKED.

"NOTHING, HONEY," MOM REPLIED. "BUT THAT'S SWEET OF YOU TO ASK. SYLVIA'S BEEN HELPING OUT."

"SYLVIA?"

MOM'S EYES DARTED TOWARD THE DOOR. I TURNED AROUND AND SAW A WELL-DRESSED, SILVER-HAIRED WOMAN WALKING IN, ALL SMILES. "THIS MUST BE YOUR DAUGHTER!" SHE EXCLAIMED, EXTENDING HER HAND. "HI, I'M SYLVIA MATTSON."

"SYLVIA IS A MEMBER OF MY SUPPORT GROUP," MOM EXPLAINED. "SHE'S GOING TO DRIVE ME HOME BECAUSE YOUR DAD IS —"

"SURPRI-I-I-ISE!"

THE SUDDEN CRY NEARLY MADE ME JUMP. BEHIND SYLVIA, FIVE OR SIX OTHER PEOPLE HAD POPPED THEIR HEADS IN THE DOOR. THEY WERE ALL GRINNING.

MOM CLASPED HER HAND TO HER MOUTH. SHE WAS AS SHOCKED AS I WAS.

ONE OF THE NEW CROWD, A MIDDLE-AGED GUY WITH A SHAVED HEAD, STEPPED INTO THE ROOM AND said, "WE ARE ALL TAKING YOU HOME, GIRL. IN STYLE!"

HE SWEPT OPEN THE CURTAINS OF MOM'S WINDOW AND GESTURED OUTSIDE.

A STRETCH LIMO WAS WAITING AT THE CURB.

MOM WAS PRACTICALLY IN TEARS. "YOU MUST BE JOKING."

THE GUY WITH THE SHAVED HEAD RAISED AN EYEBROW. "WE'RE NOT CALLED A SUPPORT GROUP FOR NOTHING, DARLING. NOW, LET'S GET YOU OUT OF HERE. THE DRIVER CHARGES BY THE MINUTE."

THE OTHERS BARGED INTO THE ROOM, LAUGHING, HUGGING MOM, HUGGING ME, HUGGING EACH OTHER, CHATTERING AWAY. THEY ALL TOLD ME THEIR NAMES, BUT I DON'T REMEMBER ANY OF THEM.

"YOU'RE COMING WITH US, RIGHT, BUNNY?" ASKED ONE OF THEM.

"SUNNY," I SAID. "AND, UH, NO. I BROUGHT MY BIKE." (I HAD BEEN PLANNING ON PUTTING IT IN THE TRUNK, BUT I DIDN'T HAVE TO TELL THEM THAT.)

MOM SEEMED HAPPY. SHE HAD LOTS OF HELP. I FELT KIND OF USELESS. SO I KISSED HER GOOD-BYE AND LEFT.

WHEN I ARRIVED HOME, I RAN TO THE

WASHING MACHINE AND SHIFTED THE MORNING WASH INTO THE DRYER. THEN I BEGAN PUTTING TOGETHER A SALAD FOR DINNER.

NEXT THING I KNEW, MOM AND THE SUPPORT GROUP WERE MARCHING THROUGH THE FRONT DOOR.

THAT WAS WHEN MOM TOLD ME I DIDN'T NEED TO MAKE A SALAD. THE GROUP HAD PLANNED TO ORDER SOME CHINESE FOOD.

"BUT IT'S A BEAUTIFUL SALAD!" MRS. MATTSON SAID. "I GUARANTEE IT'LL BE EATEN."

I WAS HAPPY TO SEE MOM. BUT, TO BE HONEST, I HAD NOT BEEN EXPECTING SNOW WHITE AND THE SEVEN DWARFS FOR DINNER.

EVERYBODY STARTED YAPPING AWAY. SO I EXCUSED MYSELF AND WENT TO MY ROOM.

WELL, THE FOOD CAME. ABOUT 20 CARTONS' WORTH. BUT WHEN I WENT DOWNSTAIRS TO GET SOME, I DECIDED MOM HAD JOINED OVEREATERS ANONYMOUS BY MISTAKE. ALMOST ALL THE FOOD WAS GONE. INCLUDING MY SALAD.

MOM WAS SITTING IN THE BIG ARMCHAIR, FACING THE SOFA. SOMEONE HAD PLACED A FEW PILLOWS AROUND HER. SHE LOOKED SO OLD AND FRAIL. SHE'D PUT ON HER WIG, BUT SOMEHOW IT MADE HER FACE LOOK SHRUNKEN.

THREE GROUP MEMBERS WERE CROWDED ON THE SOFA, LEANING TOWARD MOM. OTHERS WERE SITTING IN CHAIRS THEY'D PULLED UP BESIDE HER, AND A COUPLE SAT ON THE FLOOR AT HER FEET.

SHE WAS SURROUNDED WITH ALL KINDS OF SUPPORT. PILLOWS, LOVE, FOOD, FRIENDLY FACES.

SHE WASN'T EATING MUCH. HER PLATE WAS ON THE COFFEE TABLE, AN UNTOUCHED PILE OF NOODLES IN THE CENTER.

THE SUPPORT GROUP MEMBERS WERE A DIFFERENT STORY. THEY WERE INHALING THE FOOD.

I TRIED TO IMAGINE EACH OF THEM AS THIN AND WEAK-LOOKING AS MOM. THEY ALL MUST HAVE BEEN, AT ONE POINT.

THEN I TRIED TO PICTURE MOM ROBUST AND HUNGRY AND ENERGETIC, LIKE THEM.

THAT WAS MUCH HARDER TO DO.

I USED TO BE A POSITIVE PERSON. NOT ANYMORE.

OPTIMISM IS SUCH A STRANGE THING. IT'S LIKE A BEAUTIFUL ICE SCULPTURE ON A CLEAR, SUNNY DAY. EVERYTHING SEEMS PERFECT, BUT NO MATTER WHAT YOU DO, THE SCULPTURE STARTS TO MELT.

I THOUGHT ABOUT STAYING DOWNSTAIRS, BUT

EVERYONE WAS TALKING ABOUT TUMORS AND
HOSPITALS AND INSURANCE, SO I QUIETLY SNUCK
BACK UP TO MY ROOM.

UNFORTUNATELY, I DID NOT BRING ENOUGH
FOOD. I AM ACTUALLY LICKING THE SAUCE OFF THE
PLATE. I HOPE THERE ARE NO HIDDEN CAMERAS.

OH, WELL, I'LL HAVE A BIG BREAKFAST
TOMORROW.

GOOD NIGHT.

SATURDAY 10/25
10:34 A.M.

I AM ON A SNACK BREAK.

YES, TODAY I'M A WORKING GIRL. DAD ASKED
ME TO HELP OUT AT THE STORE. JUST ODD JOBS,
LIKE RIPPING THE COVERS OFF PAPERBACKS THAT
HAVE TO BE RETURNED TO THE PUBLISHER (SOME
STRANGE BOOKSTORE CUSTOM, I GUESS) AND
PICKING UP BOOKS THAT KIDS DROP ON THE FLOOR.

I'M GLAD I DON'T OFFICIALLY WORK FOR DAD.
HE'S A TERRIBLE BOSS. DOESN'T REALLY TELL YOU
WHAT TO DO, AND THEN, IF YOU DON'T DO WHAT
HE HAD IN MIND, HE YELLS AT YOU.

AT LEAST THAT'S WHAT HE DOES TO ME.

So right now I'm hiding from him in the Parenting section. I found a book called 20,001 Names for Baby, which gives the definition for every name you could possibly think of. I looked up Carson. It means "son of marsh dwellers."

I guess some things are better left unknown.

Okay, time out for a book review.

I discovered that Dad carries On the Road in the autobiography section. It's one of his favorite books, which raises him a notch higher on the coolness meter (and almost makes up for his incredible crankiness today). I can see why Carson likes this book. The author, Jack Kerouac, simply took off with friends, traveled across the country, and had adventures. His style is weird, and you have to read certain paragraphs about four times to understand them. But the language has this incredible rhythm. It hypnotizes you.

I wish I knew where to find Carson, so we could talk about the book. (And give it an official two thumbs-up.)

HAVE TO STOP THINKING ABOUT CARSON! BACK TO WORK!

Oops. A fresh batch of board books has landed on aisle 6. Time to clean up.

Saturday 10/25
9:27 P.M.

I HATE THEM.
I DON'T CARE WHO READS THIS ANYMORE. I HATE MOM AND DAD, AND THAT'S JUST THE WAY IT IS.

Saturday
10:49 P.M.

I was being harsh. I didn't really mean it. Well, not all the way.

I just wish that for a little while — a few minutes one morning, maybe — Mom and Dad could switch places with their old selves. Mom would be normal again, and Dad would be happy with his nice, cozy, unrenovated store. Then I could tell them what's really on my mind AND NOT FEEL SO GUILTY!

My life is a total wreck. I have stopped

BEING SUNNY WINSLOW. I HAVE MORPHED INTO A
NEW LIFE-FORM. ROBO SLAVE DAUGHTER.

YES, PARENTS, you CAN CREATE ONE IN YOUR
OWN HOME! SHE REQUIRES NO MAINTENANCE! SHE
DISAPPEARS WHEN SHE'S NOT NEEDED! SHE DOESN'T
SPEAK UNLESS SHE'S SPOKEN TO! SHE CHANGES ALL
HER PLANS AT A MOMENT'S NOTICE WHENEVER YOU
WANT HER TO! IMAGINE THE POSSIBILITIES!

I AM SICK OF IT. FIRST OF ALL, I HAVE TO
WATCH EVERY WORD THAT COMES OUT OF MY MOUTH.
DAD FLIES OFF THE HANDLE AT THE SLIGHTEST
THING. HE'S SO OVERWORKED, HE BARELY COMES
HOME. AND WHEN HE IS HOME, ALL HIS ATTENTION
IS ON MOM. I COULD DYE MY HAIR WHITE, MARCH
THROUGH THE HOUSE IN DIAPERS, AND BURP TO THE
TUNE OF "THE STAR-SPANGLED BANNER," AND HE
PROBABLY WOULDN'T NOTICE.

I TELL MYSELF TO BE REASONABLE. I TRY TO
UNDERSTAND. BUT SOMETIMES I CAN'T. SOMETIMES
MY PARENTS PUSH ME OVER THE EDGE.

LIKE TODAY.

AFTER WORK, I WAS EXHAUSTED. NEVER MIND
THAT I'M LEGALLY NOT OLD ENOUGH TO HAVE A REAL
JOB. I WAS AT THE STORE FOR FIVE HOURS, ON MY
FEET PRACTICALLY THE WHOLE TIME. I DID INVENTORY,
SWEPT THE STOCKROOM, AND HELPED CUSTOMERS.

Before lunch, I managed to avoid Dad pretty much. Afterward, I saw him too much. He yelled at me for leaving crumbs on the carpet. He yelled at me for creasing the cover of On the Road. He accused me of interrupting him while he was helping a customer. (I didn't. I said "Excuse me.")

Did I get paid? No. Did Dad at least thank me? Sort of, with a quick grunt.

But I put up with it. I knew he was under pressure. I wanted to help.

Around 3:30, I biked home. My leg muscles ached, but I didn't really care. I was excited about seeing Mom. We hadn't had "alone time" for so long.

The door was locked, and no one answered when I rang. When I let myself in, I found a note on the kitchen table:

GONE TO SUPPORT GROUP MEETING, THEN DR. MERWIN'S OFFICE FOR FOLLOW-UP VISIT. SEE YOU FOR DINNER! LOVE, MOM.

So much for alone time.

Oh, well. What I really needed was rest time anyway.

My legs creaked as I walked up to my room. I was about to plop down on my bed when I saw a shoe box on my dresser.

I hadn't put it there. I didn't even recognize the store name printed on the side.

Inside it was a pile of jewelry. Weird jewelry. I dug my fingers in and sifted through clunky wooden necklaces, enormous rings, rainbow-striped bracelets, huge brass belt buckles.

Awful. Every single piece. I mean, if I tried my hardest to create the most hideous jewelry in the world, I could not come close to the collection before me.

A folded note had been tucked in the corner. I picked it up and read:

Retro, huh? Can you believe I saved this stuff? I'll never wear it again, and I thought some of it might be back "in." Enjoy! xxxooo, Mom.

Heirlooms. A whole boxful of heirlooms. The ice sculpture was practically a puddle. I felt my headache rage back. Full blast.

I STUFFED THE NOTE AND THE JEWELRY IN THE
BOX, THEN LAY DOWN ON THE BED. I CLOSED MY
EYES, FIGURING I'D REST FOR A FEW MINUTES.

I WOKE UP TWO HOURS LATER, AT THE SOUND
OF THE BACK DOOR CLOSING.

"ANYBODY HOME?" CALLED DAD'S VOICE.

"I AM!" I CALLED BACK.

I COULD HEAR THE CLATTERING OF POTS AND
PANS IN THE KITCHEN. I SHOOK OFF MY SLEEPINESS
AND WALKED DOWNSTAIRS.

DAD WAS FURIOUSLY TURNING THE SALAD
SPINNER. "I ONLY HAVE UNTIL SEVEN OR SEVEN-
THIRTY. MY NEW ASSISTANT MANAGER CALLED IN
SICK, SO I HAVE TO GO BACK."

I ASKED IF I COULD HELP.

SEEMED LIKE AN INNOCENT QUESTION. WELL,
NOT TO DAD.

HE OPENED THE SPINNER AND BEGAN RIPPING
THE LETTUCE WITH HIS HANDS. "I WAS KIND OF
HOPING . . ." RIP! "SOME DINNER . . ." RIP!
"WOULD HAVE BEEN PREPARED." RIP!

"SORRY, DAD --"

"WEEKEND HOMEWORK AGAIN?"

"NO, I WAS JUST RESTING."

DAD FLUNG THE LEAVES INTO A GLASS BOWL.
"YOU KNOW, WE'RE ALL VERY BUSY HERE, HONEY --"

"I KNOW, DAD!" I OPENED THE FRIDGE AND TOOK OUT A BOTTLE OF JUICE.

"YOU DON'T HAVE TO SPEAK TO ME THAT WAY, SUNNY --"

"I JUST SAID --"

"IN A FAMILY WE ALL HAVE TO PULL OUR OWN WEIGHT --"

DINGDONG!

"I'LL GET IT!"

"I'LL GET IT!"

I RAN OUT FIRST. I COULD NOT STAND BEING IN THAT KITCHEN ONE MORE SECOND.

MOM WAS AT THE DOOR, ARM IN ARM WITH MRS. MATTSON. WE ALL CHATTED FOR AWHILE AS I HELPED MOM INSIDE.

DAD SWOOPED INTO THE FRONT HALL, WEARING A KITCHEN APRON. "WELCOME HOME!"

HE AND MOM HUGGED, SO I LET GO. THEN THEY WALKED INTO THE KITCHEN TOGETHER. I TAGGED ALONG.

"WE'RE NOT QUITE READY FOR DINNER," DAD SAID. "I PUT SOUP ON THE STOVE AND I'M MICROWAVING SOME LEFTOVERS. I'LL HELP YOU TO THE BATHROOM, WHILE SUNNY DOES HER SHARE IN THE KITCHEN."

MY SHARE?

I GRITTED MY TEETH. I WALKED INTO THE
KITCHEN AND CALMLY STABBED A CUCUMBER TO
DEATH. THEN I THREW TOGETHER A SALAD AND SET
THE TABLE.

BE GRATEFUL, I TOLD MYSELF. THIS WILL BE
OUR FIRST FAMILY MEAL IN AGES.

"SO," MOM BEGAN AS WE SAT DOWN, "WHAT
DID YOU THINK, SUNNY? CAN YOU BELIEVE I
ACTUALLY WORE THAT JEWELRY BACK THEN?"

DAD SAID SOMETHING SO DUMB I NEARLY
CHOKED. HE KIND OF CHUCKLED ABOUT HOW IN STYLE
ALL THAT KIND OF STUFF IS.

ALL I SAID WAS, "IT'S A LITTLE DIFFERENT,
DAD," AND HE LOOKED AT ME AS IF I'D JUST SAID
I WAS GOING TO BOMB HIS STORE.

"DON'T WORRY, I WON'T BE OFFENDED IF YOU
THROW THEM OUT, SUNNY," MOM SAID. "I JUST
THOUGHT YOU'D WANT TO LOOK AT THEM.
ACTUALLY, I THINK YOU'D REALLY LIKE MY
BEAUTIFUL OLD MADRAS COTTON DRESSES --"

"UH, THANKS, MOM," I REPLIED, "BUT YOU
DON'T HAVE TO LEAVE ME . . . SURPRISES. REALLY."

"OH, I DON'T MIND --"

"IN FACT, I DON'T WANT YOU TO."

I HAD TO SAY IT THAT PLAINLY. MOM JUST
WASN'T GETTING IT.

She sighed. "You know, during all these hospital stays, I think about all the clutter in my life. I've become obsessed with cleaning up. That's all. And I figure, if you can use any of it, why not?"

"Well, it's just that -- those gifts, they're so --" Morbid, I wanted to say. "Unfashionable. I mean, not age-appropriate or whatever."

That was when Dad broke in and started accusing me of not being grateful.

"I AM grateful," I snapped. "I just don't want any heirlooms, okay? I don't. I'm allowed to say how I feel."

Dad's face was turning red. "We don't need to be told what you are and aren't allowed to say in this house. This is an issue of manners, not free speech --"

"What's the difference? No one listens to me anyway!"

"Sunshine, you are out of line!" Dad thundered. "At a time like this, when your mother is ill, and I'm under pressure at the store, the least you can do is help make our home environment pleasant!"

I stood up from the table. "You want a pleasant environment? Then renovate! Hire a

WHOLE TEAM OF DAUGHTERS YOU CAN BOSS AROUND,
AND THEN SEND THEM HOME SO YOU DON'T HAVE
TO TALK TO THEM."

I DIDN'T EVEN HEAR A RESPONSE. THE ONLY
SOUNDS I WAS AWARE OF WERE MY FOOTSTEPS ON
THE STAIRS AND THE SLAMMING OF MY BEDROOM
DOOR.

SUNDAY 10/26
10:05 A.M.

I THOUGHT I'D WAKE UP IN A BETTER MOOD.
I DIDN'T.

DAD SERVED MOM BREAKFAST IN BED TODAY.
I ENDED UP EATING CHEERIOS ALONE IN THE
KITCHEN.

I THOUGHT ABOUT APOLOGIZING TO MOM. SHE
DIDN'T DESERVE MY OUTBURST YESTERDAY, REALLY.
BUT IF I DID, I'D HAVE TO FACE DAD TOO.

FORGET THAT.

TO BE HONEST, I DIDN'T WANT TO BE
AROUND THE HOUSE AT ALL TODAY.

DAD WAS GOING TO STAY HOME FOR HALF THE
DAY TO BE WITH MOM. AND MR. SCHAFER WAS

COMING OVER WITH CAROL TO BRING MOM A GOURMET LUNCH. OKAY, SO IF I WANTED TO SEE MOM ALONE, I'D HAVE TO WAIT UNTIL THIS EVENING. UNTIL THEN, THIS HOUSE WAS GOING TO BE TOO CROWDED.

"I'M GOING OVER TO MAGGIE'S FOR AWHILE," I ANNOUNCED.

MOM AND DAD WERE DEEP IN CONVERSATION. THEY SAID OKAY IN MIDSENTENCE.

I PACKED MY BLADES AND A BATHING SUIT, AND I LEFT.

THIS BUS STOP IS MUCH MORE CROWDED ON THE WEEKEND THAN DURING THE WEEK. I ALMOST GOT ON THE ONE TO ANAHEIM BY MISTAKE. IT'S A GOOD THING I DIDN'T.

THE BUS TO VENICE BEACH IS DUE IN TWO MINUTES. I THINK I SEE IT.

ALREADY I'M IN A <u>MUCH</u> BETTER MOOD. IT'S A PERFECT BEACH DAY.

IF MOM AND DAD CALL MAGGIE'S HOUSE, I'M IN BIG TROUBLE. BUT I'M SURE THEY WON'T EVEN THINK OF IT.

ROBO SLAVE DAUGHTER -- OUT OF SIGHT, OUT OF MIND.

SUNDAY
11:53 A.M., VENICE BEACH

I REALLY HAVE TO DO THIS MORE OFTEN. I AM HAVING THE BEST DAY!

I THOUGHT I'D BE NERVOUS SNEAKING AWAY. I WASN'T. WHEN I ARRIVED HERE, I FELT AS IF I WERE RETURNING TO A FAVORITE OLD SPOT.

VENICE BEACH IS SO COOL ON THE WEEKEND. I BLADED UP AND DOWN THE BOARDWALK, BUT I KEPT STOPPING TO SEE THINGS.

A GUY JUGGLING BEACH UMBRELLAS. A WOMEN'S WEIGHT LIFTING CONTEST. A DOG FRISBEE THROW. JET-SKIING. PARASAILING.

I BODY-SURFED. I DRANK A PAPAYA SHAKE. NOW I'M STRETCHED OUT ON MY BLANKET, OCCASIONALLY READING ON THE ROAD.

THE WEATHER IS PERFECT. THE SUN IS TOASTING ME LIGHTLY, BUT THE COOL BREEZE MAKES IT COMFORTABLE.

YOU KNOW WHAT? I AM NOT DEVASTATED THAT CARSON ISN'T HERE. YES, I LOOKED FOR HIM. NO, NOT A TRACE. I WAS PRETTY UPSET AT FIRST, BUT NOW I FEEL: IF HE SHOWS UP, FINE. IF NOT, IT WON'T KILL ME. I LOVE BEING ALONE.

I ABSOLUTELY MUST HAVE ONE MORE RIDE
ON THE WAVES. IF I DO IT NOW, I'LL HAVE
ENOUGH TIME TO DRY BEFORE THE BUS RIDE
HOME.

SUNDAY

2:07 P.M.

THE HOUSE WAS SILENT AND GLOOMY, AS
ALWAYS, WHEN I ARRIVED. MOM WAS ASLEEP IN HER
ROOM.

THE FIRST THING I DID WAS CALL MAGGIE.
HER DAD ANSWERED AND SAID SHE WAS OUT
SHOPPING WITH HER MOM. I KNOW HE WOULD HAVE
TOLD ME IF MOM AND DAD HAD CALLED HIM.

I HAD PULLED IT OFF. COOL.

I TOOK A QUICK SHOWER, THEN CALLED DAWN.
I WAS REALLY MISSING HER.

"SUNNY!" SHE EXCLAIMED. "OH, I WISH I COULD
HAVE COME TO LUNCH WITH MY PARENTS AND YOUR
PARENTS! I WAS SOOOO BUSY! MOM AND DAD SAID
YOU WEREN'T THERE EITHER."

I MADE SOME DUMB EXCUSE. SHE TOLD ME SHE
WAS GOING TO HER STEPGRANDPARENTS' FOR
DINNER. AND THAT WAS THAT.

OKAY, SO I DIDN'T TELL HER ABOUT THE BEACH. BUT SHE DIDN'T ASK.

AND I DO NOT FEEL GUILTY.

MONDAY 10/27
3 P.M.

WHY DOES EVERYTHING HAVE TO CHANGE SO FAST? WHY COULDN'T IT HAVE STAYED THE WAY IT WAS LAST EVENING?

I MEAN, EVERYTHING SEEMED COOL. AFTER MOM WOKE UP, SHE ASKED ABOUT MY HOMEWORK (WHICH I HADN'T STARTED YET), BUT I CHANGED THE SUBJECT. FORTUNATELY SHE DID NOT ASK ABOUT MY TRIP TO MAGGIE'S HOUSE.

DAD CAME HOME FOR DINNER, THEN WENT BACK TO THE STORE.

YOUR BASIC BORING EVENING. I'LL TAKE THAT OVER ARGUING ANY DAY. BESIDES, WHEN I STARTED TO GET BUMMED, I WOULD JUST THINK OF MY LITTLE SECRET.

IT'S AMAZING HOW WELL THAT WORKS.

I REMEMBERED MY HOMEWORK AT BEDTIME, AND I STARTED A BOOK REPORT ABOUT ON THE ROAD. BUT THAT MADE ME THINK OF CARSON, SO I

TRIED TO SKETCH HIS FACE BY MEMORY. AND EVENTUALLY I DRIFTED OFF.

IT COULD HAVE BEEN MY FIRST FULL NIGHT'S SLEEP IN WEEKS.

IT WASN'T.

AROUND 3:00 A.M., MOM'S VOICE WOKE ME UP. IT WAS COMING FROM HER ROOM.

I WENT TO MY DOOR. DAD WAS IN HIS PAJAMAS, HEADING FOR THE BATHROOM. HE LOOKED SO GROGGY, HIS EYES WERE SLITS.

"I'M GETTING YOUR MOM SOME WATER," HE INFORMED ME. "SHE'S NOT SLEEPING WELL. GO TALK TO HER."

I WENT INTO THE BEDROOM. MOM WAS ON HER SIDE, HER EYES WIDE OPEN. "HI, SUNNY. IS IT COLD IN HERE?"

"A LITTLE." I PULLED UP A COTTON BLANKET THAT WAS FOLDED NEAR HER FEET.

DAD CAME SHUFFLING BACK IN AND GAVE MOM A PAPER CUPFUL OF WATER. SHE SWALLOWED IT FAST AND THEN SAID, "WILL YOU READ TO ME, PAUL? THAT ALWAYS PUTS ME TO SLEEP."

A JOKE, I THINK, BUT DAD DIDN'T LAUGH.

FIRST HE READ TO HER WHILE I WENT BACK TO BED. THEN HE STARTED FALLING ASLEEP, SO HE CALLED ME IN TO READ TO HER.

Soon Mom fell asleep too.
But I didn't.

Breakfast this morning was brutal.
My eyes were closed through most of
it. My skin stung from sunburn. I could
barely eat. Mom and Dad were upstairs, fast
asleep.

Or so I thought.

I was just about to leave for school
when Dad called down: "Sunny, could you get
Dr. Merwin on the phone? Your mom's running
a fever, and I can't get through!"

I picked up the kitchen extension. I must
have gotten a busy signal 20 times before
the phone finally rang.

When I explained everything to Dr.
Merwin, he said, "Bring her right in."

Next thing I knew, Dad and I were
helping Mom out to the car. She was hunched
over and coughing.

Dad drove Mom to the hospital, and I
ran to school. I arrived in the middle of
homeroom.

Mr. Leavitt yelled at me. I yawned. He
yelled even louder.

I FELL ASLEEP IN SCIENCE CLASS. MS. CARTER WAS NOT AMUSED.

MS. NEWELL WASN'T EITHER, WHEN I TOLD HER I HADN'T FINISHED MY BOOK REPORT.

MR. HACKETT GAVE ME ANOTHER LONG LECTURE ABOUT COMMITMENT. I COULDN'T HELP YAWNING IN THE MIDDLE OF IT, AND HE SENT ME TO THE PRINCIPAL'S OFFICE AGAIN, WHERE MR. DEAN SYMPATHIZED WITH ME SO MUCH I WANTED TO PUKE.

I FLEW OUT OF THAT OFFICE AND RAN RIGHT INTO DAWN AND MAGGIE, WHO WERE TALKING TO DUCKY IN THE HALLWAY.

I WAS TOTALLY BLOWN OUT. I DID NOT KNOW WHAT WAS GOING TO COME OUT OF MY MOUTH.

"WHAT WERE YOU DOING IN THERE?" DAWN ASKED.

"YOU DIDN'T HEAR? ABOUT MR. DEAN AND ME?" I SAID, RAISING AN EYEBROW. "IT'S SERIOUS."

DUCKY BURST OUT LAUGHING. DAWN BLUSHED.

MAGGIE, HOWEVER, WAS STARING AT ME. "HOW DID YOUR FACE GET SO BURNED?"

"HE HAS A DECK OUT BEHIND HIS OFFICE," I SAID, WALKING AWAY. "WE WERE SUNBATHING."

DUMB QUESTIONS, DUMB ANSWERS.

WELL, MAGGIE DID NOT SPEAK TO ME THE

REST OF THE DAY. THAT GIRL CANNOT TAKE A JOKE.

DAWN KEPT GIVING ME WEIRD LOOKS IN THE HALLWAY.

I GUESS DUCKY HAS A SENSE OF HUMOR. BEFORE LAST PERIOD, I SAW HIM IN THE HALLWAY AND HE WAS AS FRIENDLY AS COULD BE. "YOU WERE AT THE BEACH THIS WEEKEND, HUH?" HE SAID.

"YUP."

"ME TOO. NEXT TIME YOU GO, CALL ME. I'LL GIVE YOU A RIDE. WE CAN ALL GO -- DAWN AND MAGGIE TOO."

WHAT COULD I SAY? IT WAS NICE OF HIM, BUT I COULDN'T SAY YES. AND I COULDN'T EXACTLY TELL HIM THE WHOLE TRUTH. SO I SAID, "WELL, I DIDN'T GO TO THAT BEACH."

BEFORE HE ASKED ANOTHER QUESTION, I WAS GONE.

AFTER SCHOOL I AVOIDED ALL OF THEM -- MAGGIE, DAWN, AND DUCKY.

WAIT A SEC. THE ANSWERING MACHINE IS BLINKING.

OH, GREAT.

MORE LATER.

WHY IS HE ALWAYS YELLING AT ME?

I CAN'T TAKE IT ANYMORE..

HE ACTS AS IF EVERYTHING IS MY FAULT. HE GETS SO ANGRY ABOUT LIFE AND THEN HE TAKES IT OUT ON ME.

EVEN THAT MESSAGE -- THAT ANSWERING MACHINE MESSAGE I STARTED WRITING ABOUT BEFORE -- EVEN THAT WAS RUDE.

"PACK A BAG AND TAKE IT TO YOUR MOM. SHE'S IN THE HOSPITAL WITH PNEUMONIA." CLICK.

THAT WAS IT.

I MEAN, HIT ME OVER THE HEAD A LITTLE HARDER, WHY DON'T YOU?

NOT ONLY THAT. DIDN'T HE CARE? SURE DIDN'T SOUND LIKE IT.

ME? I CARED.

CANCER. BRONCHITIS. PNEUMONIA.

WHAT NEXT?

I PUT TOGETHER A BACKPACK IN RECORD TIME. I FLEW TO THE HOSPITAL ON MY BIKE. I WAS NEARLY KILLED WHEN I WENT THROUGH A STOP SIGN.

MOM WAS ON OXYGEN WHEN I ARRIVED. SHE COULDN'T REALLY TALK, SO I GAVE HER THE PACK,

HELD HER HAND WHILE BABBLING ON ABOUT WHO KNOWS WHAT, AND LEFT.

I WAS PRETTY CALM ON THE WAY HOME, UNTIL I PASSED CITY OF ANGELS POTTERY STUDIO. I THOUGHT ABOUT HOW I USED TO VISIT MOM THERE AFTER SCHOOL WHEN I WAS LITTLE. THAT MADE ME DEPRESSED.

SOON EVERYTHING -- STORES, STREETS, SMELLS -- BEGAN REMINDING ME OF MOM WHEN SHE WAS HEALTHY.

THAT DID IT.

I STARTED CRYING. LIKE A BABY.

I NEVER CRY. WHAT IS HAPPENING TO ME?

I WAS ACTING AS IF MOM WOULD NEVER BE HEALTHY AGAIN. I WAS GIVING UP.

WHEN I ARRIVED HOME, THE HOUSE WAS DARK AND EMPTY. IT WAS LIKE WALKING INTO A ROOM WITHOUT AIR.

I HAD TO TALK TO SOMEONE.

DAWN? NOT AFTER THE WAY SHE WAS ACTING TOWARD ME TODAY.

NOT MAGGIE, EITHER. SHE WAS MAD.

I DIDN'T KNOW DUCKY WELL ENOUGH.

SO I STARTED WRITING. THEN DAD HAD TO COME HOME AND START BOSSING ME AROUND.

HE'S MAD AT THE DIRT IN THE HOUSE. HE'S MAD BECAUSE HE HAS NO CLEAN SHIRTS. NO RAISINS OR NUTS IN THE HOUSE.

AND IT'S ALL MY FAULT, OF COURSE.

I DON'T KNOW WHAT TO DO.

I THINK I WILL EXPLODE.

TUESDAY 10/28
9:30 A.M.

GOOD-BYE.

OFF TO YOU-KNOW-WHERE.

TUESDAY
2:35 P.M., VENICE BEACH

STOP SHAKING, WINSLOW.

WRITE IT ALL. EVERY LAST DETAIL.

SAVOR IT, KID.

OKAY. THIS MORNING. THE MINUTE I ARRIVED HERE, I STRAPPED ON MY BLADES AND TOOK OFF. THE BOARDWALK WAS SO OPEN. MUCH LESS CROWDED THAN IT HAD BEEN ON SUNDAY. I WAS FLYING.

I WASN'T THINKING ABOUT MOM OR DAD OR SCHOOL. MY HEAD WAS CLEARING BY THE SECOND.

I DID NOT EXPECT CARSON TO SPEED BY ME IN THE OPPOSITE DIRECTION.

I TURNED AND NEARLY HURTLED INTO A CROWD OF WEIGHT LIFTERS.

"HEY!" I CALLED OUT.

CARSON SPUN AROUND. HE GAVE ME A BLANK LOOK.

"SUNNY!" I REMINDED HIM. "REMEMBER?"

CRRRRRACK! LIGHTNING SPLIT THE AIR. THUNDER SHOOK THE EARTH. THE SKIES OPENED AND A CHOIR OF ANGELS DESCENDED.

WELL, MAYBE NOT. BUT CARSON DID SMILE. THAT WAS COOL.

HE SKATED CLOSER. "YOU BROUGHT YOUR BLADES."

"I LIVE IN THEM," I REPLIED. (A LIE, YES, BUT IT JUST SEEMED THE RIGHT THING TO SAY.)

"YEAH. ME TOO." THAT SMILE WAS A KILLER. "WELL, SEE YOU."

"WAIT! I WAS ABOUT TO GO THAT WAY TOO."

CARSON NODDED. "UH-HUH. WELL, ACTUALLY, I WAS GOING TO GET SOME JOE."

"JOE? I LOVE JOE!" (NOT.)

"COOL." HE SHRUGGED AND HEADED TOWARD THE JAVA VOOM CAFE.

I SKATED BEHIND HIM TO AN OUTDOOR TABLE ON A SMALL TERRACE. A WAITER CAME RIGHT OVER TO US. "CUP OF JOE," CARSON ORDERED. "LARGE."

"SAME," I SAID.

WHEN THE WAITER RETURNED, HE PLACED TWO STEAMING, BLACK, AWFUL-SMELLING CUPS BEFORE US.

"NICE PLACE," I SAID. (DUH.)

CARSON NODDED AND STARED OUT TO SEA. HE LOOKED TOTALLY RELAXED. AS IF I WEREN'T THERE.

I SAT FORWARD. I SAT BACK. I BLEW ON MY COFFEE. I SMILED. I NOTICED HOW HUGE MY FEET LOOKED. I REMEMBERED THE PIMPLE I'D SEEN THIS MORNING NEAR MY LEFT NOSTRIL.

WHY WASN'T HE SAYING ANYTHING?

FINALLY, AFTER ABOUT 17 HOURS, HE SIPPED HIS COFFEE AND SAID, "NO SCHOOL?"

"NAHHHH. I'M JUST -- WELL, TODAY IS -- WE DIDN'T -- " I TOOK A DEEP BREATH. "I'M CUTTING."

CARSON LAUGHED. "ALL RIIIGHT!"

NICE TO KNOW SOMEONE APPROVED.

"I MEAN, SOMETIMES YOU JUST CAN'T GO," I SAID BOLDLY. "IF THEY DON'T LIKE IT, TOO BAD."

"THEY PROBABLY DON'T CARE, ANYWAY," HE REMARKED.

He sipped his coffee. I sipped mine.

He looked out to the ocean.

I nearly had a heart attack.

The coffee was awful! ALL coffee is awful. What possessed me to order some and actually drink it? I must have been insane.

I started coughing.

"You okay?" Carson asked.

"Uh-huh," I said. "Went down the wrong pipe."

Carson quickly fetched a cup of water for me.

I swigged it down. "Thanks. Strong coffee."

"Tastes like mud to me," Carson remarked.

"Me too!"

Carson spilled his cup onto the brick floor. He didn't even look to see if anyone was watching.

I frankly didn't care either. Over it went.

Both of us started laughing.

"Out of here," Carson said, standing up.

He pulled a few bills out of his pocket and slapped them on the table. Together we bladed down the boardwalk, past the shops. Carson showed me how to do a few spins. I

TRIED TO IMITATE HIM AND PLUNGED INTO THE
SAND.

CARSON FELL DOWN BESIDE ME.

WE STAYED THERE, GIGGLING AT FIRST, THEN
JUST LYING STILL. PEOPLE WHIZZED BY US ON
SKATES, BIKES, AND SKATEBOARDS, BUT WE DIDN'T
PAY THEM ANY ATTENTION.

"I WANT TO GET MY FEET WET," CARSON
SUDDENLY ANNOUNCED.

WE TOOK OFF OUR BLADES, SLUNG THEM OVER
OUR SHOULDERS, AND WALKED TOWARD THE WATER.
JUST BEFORE THE SURF, WHERE THE SAND IS WET
AND FIRM, WE TURNED LEFT.

AS WE WALKED, WE WATCHED A GROUP OF
LITTLE BIRDS RUN AFTER EACH RECEDING WAVE, ONLY
TO BE CHASED BACK BY THE NEXT ONE. "WHY DO
THEY DO THAT?" I ASKED.

"SANDPIPERS," CARSON SAID. "THEY EAT THE
ALGAE LEFT BY THE WAVE. THEY DON'T HAVE
MUCH TIME, SO THEY HAVE TO GRAB WHAT THEY
CAN."

"THAT'S WHAT MY DAD SAYS ABOUT PEOPLE."

"WHAT? THEY EAT ALGAE?"

"NOOOO!"

CARSON WAS GRINNING. I PUNCHED HIM IN THE
SHOULDER.

At that moment I felt really close to him. I linked my arm in his. He didn't mind.

I realized I hadn't told him a word about myself -- or at least a truthful word.

"Carson," I said. "My name isn't Camilla."

"I know. It's Sunny."

I stopped in my tracks. "How do you know?"

"You said so, back on the boardwalk."

Aggggh. I could feel my face turning red. "Well, see, I guess Camilla is sort of a -- I don't know, a --"

"Road name."

"Huh?"

"Lots of people use them. People who hike the Appalachian Trail, guys who hop trains. Me."

"You? Why?"

"Because people might recognize my real name on a Wanted poster."

"What?"

"Joke," Carson said with a laugh. "You know what's the coolest thing in the world? Walking into a strange town and starting a life from scratch. Finding a place to live, work, friends . . . it's like you're a new person.

Sometimes you need a new name too. I don't know why. It just feels right. I've been Neal Cassady, Dean Moriarty —"

"From On the Road!" I exclaimed.

Carson looked impressed. "It's practically my bible."

"So, how do I know Carson's your real name?"

"You don't," Carson said with a sly grin.

I gave him a shove. "You can't fool everybody, you know. I guess you're not going to tell me anything about yourself."

"What do you want to know?"

"Your age, where you're from, how you got here, your last name . . ."

"Seventeen, Cleveland, hitching, and it doesn't matter."

"Okay, I'll guess the rest. You graduated high school, and you're really not as tough as you sound. Your mom and dad gave you money to travel around the country for a year."

"I didn't graduate. I just left school. Who needs it? I've had plenty of jobs since I left, and I didn't have a diploma."

"My parents would kill me if I tried that."

Carson snorted a laugh. "My mom hardly noticed. She probably just discovered I'm gone. Her boyfriend's thrilled, I'll bet."

"That's so sad, Carson."

"It was, when I was there. I don't think about it anymore."

"So I guess that makes you a runaway."

"A dropout runaway," Carson said dryly. "You afraid of me now?"

"No! Why would I be?"

Carson shrugged. "You look like you come from a nice, normal family."

"Oh, puh-leeze!" I cringed. "You don't know! My dad is never home. My mom -- well, she can't really function. She's in the hospital all the time. And when she's not, she's with this support group. I'm, like, invisible in the house, until work needs to be done. Then I'm the hired help. Some life, huh? I don't have one. My house is this big prison. And don't get me started with school. That's even worse."

It really, REALLY felt good to get that out of my system. You know what I liked best about Carson? He didn't judge. He didn't tell me what to do.

He just listened.

We walked silently for awhile. A wave rolled over our feet, carrying a perfect white seashell. Carson picked it up and handed it to me. "It's for good luck."

I turned it over. Its smooth inner wall shone in the sun. "It's beautiful," I said.

I rested my head on Carson's shoulder and listened to the gulls. I was kind of hoping he'd ask more about me, but he didn't.

Which was fine, to tell the truth. I didn't want to admit my age. And I would have, if he'd asked. I was feeling very open and truthful.

Oh, well, that will be my secret.

We were approaching the cafe again. I could see a clock through the window and my heart sank. The bus I wanted to take was going to arrive in a few minutes.

"I have to go," I said. "Maybe we can do this again?"

"Sure."

"What would be a good time? Maybe Friday morning?"

Carson gave me a half smile and shook his

HEAD. "NO PLANS. I HATE PLANS. IF YOU WANT
TO COME AND HANG OUT, COOL. I'M HERE A
LOT."

"OKAY. THEN MAYBE I'LL SEE YOU."

"I HOPE SO."

AND THAT WAS THAT. CARSON WAVED TO ME
AS HE BLADED AWAY.

WELL, I WAS WRONG ABOUT THE BUS. I'D
MISSED IT. NOW I'M WAITING FOR THE NEXT ONE.

I'VE HAD LOTS OF TIME TO WRITE AND THINK.
I'M A LITTLE NUMB. BUT I AM CALMER THAN
WHEN I STARTED WRITING THIS.

SO WHAT NOW? THAT'S THE BIG QUESTION.

I'M FULL OF STRANGE FEELINGS.

I HAVE NEVER, EVER BEEN MORE ATTRACTED TO
A GUY. I HAVE NEVER MET ANYONE AS EXCITING. I
COULD SPEND WEEKS AND WEEKS WITH CARSON AND
NOT GET BORED.

DO I LOVE HIM?

I DON'T KNOW.

I'M NOT DYING TO KISS HIM AND TRADE RINGS
OR WHATEVER. I DON'T WANT TO E-MAIL AND CALL
HIM EVERY DAY AND GO ON DATES EVERY WEEKEND.
I MEAN, LET'S FACE IT. HE'S A RUNAWAY. HE'S A
LONER.

HE'S JUST LIKE ME.

EVERY WORD HE SAID COULD HAVE COME FROM MY MOUTH. THE DIFFERENCE? HE'S REALLY <u>DONE</u> SOMETHING ABOUT THE WAY HE FEELS. ME? I'M HEADING BACK HOME, READY TO COVER MYSELF WITH EXCUSES.

SO WHAT IS IT I'M FEELING? IS THERE A WORD FOR SOMETHING MORE THAN LOVE?

I'LL THINK OF ONE ON THE RIDE HOME. HERE COMES THE BUS.

WEDNESDAY 11/5

10:04 A.M., STUDY HALL

PALO CITY HOSPITAL

To Whom It May Concern:
Sunny Winslow missed three days of school within the week (October 28, 30, and November 4), because of her commitments to the health maintenance of her mother. Please excuse her without academic penalty.
Sincerely Yours,
Dr. Michael C. Mervin, M.D.

This note saved my life today. Printing the letterhead was easy. The handwriting was the hard part. Fortunately, Mom had a prescription from Dr. Merwin lying around, and this is exactly how terrible his handwriting looks.

I give myself an A+ in forgery and espionage. (Maybe I've finally found my true calling.)

For my journal writing, though, I deserve a big, fat F. It's been one whole week since I last wrote, so I have lots of catch-up.

Here goes. First of all, Mom's feeling better. She's home. She spends a lot of time on the phone, and Sylvia drives her around all day. (Sylvia's middle name is Loves-to-Shop.)

Dad? Well, all the new windows in his store were measured wrong, and they're too short. He went ballistic. In fact, now I'm afraid he's going to have a heart attack. I have hardly seen him this last week. (I think he's making the new windows himself.)

Now back to the big news: my transformation into a world-class forger.

I had no choice. My teachers were really

GETTING ON MY CASE. WELL, MOST OF THEM. MR. HACKETT FINALLY RAN OUT OF PITYING LOOKS AND STARTED GETTING ANGRY. HE WAS THE ONE WHO DEMANDED A NOTE.

DAWN AND MAGGIE KNOW SOMETHING'S UP. THEY'RE BEING KIND OF DISTANT, AS IF THEY'RE NOT SURE HOW TO APPROACH ME.

FRANKLY, I DON'T CARE WHAT PEOPLE THINK ANYMORE. I'VE ENJOYED ALL MY TRIPS TO VENICE BEACH THIS WEEK. ESPECIALLY SATURDAY'S, WHEN I BROUGHT A SURFBOARD. (I TOLD MOM I WAS GOING TO THE LOCAL BEACH. SHE OFFERED TO DRIVE ME, BUT I TOLD HER DUCKY WOULD.)

I AM A HORRIBLE, TWO-FACED LIAR. BUT I'M GETTING USED TO IT. IT'S BETTER THAN BEING A MISERABLE, SULKING, DEPRESSED GIRL WHO HANGS AROUND HOME AND BURDENS EVERYBODY. NOW, WHEN I'M FEELING BAD -- OFF TO THE BEACH, COME HOME SMILING.

I STILL CAN'T STAND BEING IN THIS HOUSE. BUT IT'S NICE TO HAVE AN ESCAPE.

AND I'M NOT HARMING A SOUL.

IT HELPS THAT CARSON HAS BEEN AT THE BEACH EVERY SINGLE TIME I'VE BEEN THERE. MY FAVORITE VISIT WAS THE ONE ON SATURDAY.

CARSON'S EYES WENT WIDE WHEN HE SAW MY
SURFBOARD.

"NICE BOARD," HE SAID.

"DO YOU SURF?" I ASKED.

"SURE."

"THEN RENT ONE."

"NAHH. I TWISTED MY ANKLE."

"BUT YOU CAN BLADE?"

CARSON'S FACE TURNED BEET-RED. I BURST
OUT LAUGHING. "I HEAR THE SURF'S GREAT UP
THERE IN CLEVELAND."

"WELL, I -- I DIDN'T SAY I WAS GREAT AT
IT --"

"HAVE YOU BEEN ON A BOARD IN YOUR LIFE,
CARSON?"

HE LOOKED OUT INTO THE DISTANCE, AS IF HE'D
SPOTTED SOME RARE SPECIES OF PACIFIC SANDPIPER.
"UH . . . WELL, NO."

"COME ON, I'LL TEACH YOU."

I GRABBED HIS HAND AND PULLED HIM TOWARD
THE SURF. AT FIRST HE SPUTTERED AND
PROTESTED, BUT HE CAME.

WELL, GUESS WHAT? CARSON NO-LASTNAME IS
NOT PERFECT. IN FACT, IF I WERE TO GRADE HIM
ON BEGINNERS' SURFBOARD TECHNIQUE, I'D GIVE
HIM A D. HE FLAILED HIS ARMS, HE COULDN'T

CENTER HIMSELF ON THE BOARD, HE COULDN'T
STAND, AND HIS TIMING WAS ATROCIOUS.

I MUST SAY, THOUGH, HE WAS A GOOD SPORT.
EACH TIME HE FELL, HE GOT BACK UP AND
MUTTERED SOMETHING LIKE, "GOTTA SHIFT MY
WEIGHT," OR "THAT WAS CLOSER." HE ONLY BECAME
ANGRY ONCE OR TWICE, BUT THAT WAS BECAUSE I
LAUGHED AT HIM.

HE WAS SO DETERMINED.

AND HE WAS SO CUTE, I COULDN'T STAND IT.

AFTERWARD WE SAT AT JAVA VOOM AGAIN.
(THIS TIME I HAD HERBAL TEA.) WE SPENT ABOUT
AN HOUR MAKING UP STORIES ABOUT THE PEOPLE
WHO PASSED BY. WE WERE HOWLING.

I FEEL SO COMFORTABLE WITH CARSON NOW --
AS IF I'VE KNOWN HIM MY WHOLE LIFE. WE FINISH
EACH OTHER'S SENTENCES. I KNOW JUST BY THE
LOOK IN HIS EYE WHAT HE'S THINKING.

SO WHY WON'T HE TELL ME HIS LAST NAME?
OR ANYTHING PERSONAL, FOR THAT MATTER. HE
LETS ME IN AND LETS ME IN, AND THEN -- WHAM!
THE DOOR SLAMS IN MY FACE.

I DIDN'T EVEN BOTHER ASKING HIM QUESTIONS
TODAY. BUT I STILL WANT TO KNOW EVERYTHING.
I'M STARTING TO DREAM ABOUT HIM NOW. THIS IS

GUESS WHO INTERRUPTED MY LAST ENTRY? MS. KRUEGER. SHE JUST WALKED INTO STUDY HALL AND SAT DOWN NEXT TO ME.

"SUNNY," SHE SAID, "I HAVE BEEN TRYING TO DECIDE HOW TO APPROACH YOU. YOU CAME UP AT OUR DEPARTMENTAL MEETING."

I ALMOST LAUGHED. ME? A TOPIC OF DISCUSSION AMONG TEACHERS THAT WEREN'T EVEN MINE?

OH, WELL. AFTER THAT PARTY, MS. KRUEGER HAD SAID SHE'D BE KEEPING AN EYE ON DUCKY, DAWN, AND ME. SHE WAS TRUE TO HER WORD.

"I GUESS I MUST BE PRETTY INTERESTING AND COMPLEX," I SAID.

MS. KRUEGER LAUGHED. "WELL, YOU'RE HUMAN. AND I FIGURE IT'S TIME THE TEACHERS STOPPED TREATING YOU LIKE A FRAGILE TEACUP. WHAT'S UP?"

"UP?" I SHRUGGED. "YOU KNOW . . ."

"YOU'RE MISSING SCHOOL."

I STARTED TO MENTION DR. MERWIN, BUT MS. KRUEGER CUT ME OFF. "MS. NEWELL SHOWED ME THE NOTE," SHE SAID. "SIGNED DR. MICHAEL

Merwin, M.D. I don't know of any doctors who write both Doctor and M.D. with their names."

"Oh." I felt about three inches tall. "I wonder why he does that."

"You know, some teachers don't believe that Dr. Merwin wrote that. But I told them I didn't believe you would do something illegal."

"Illegal?"

"Look, Sunny. I can't climb into your head and know what's going on in there. But you need to go to school. And you can use the school. Use your friends. Use me. I will sit and listen to anything you want to say. Anything. But I'm not going to beg you, and I'm not going to drag you. This is just an open invitation, no expiration date."

I nodded. I mean, that was nice of her, but what was I supposed to say? I'll never take her up on the offer.

Ms. Krueger stood up with a smile, touched my arm gently, and left.

Now what? She knows I had forged the letter. Do the other teachers? Are they all humoring me?

I WAS STILL IN SHOCK WHEN I LEFT STUDY HALL.

I DIDN'T EVEN NOTICE DUCKY WHEN I PASSED HIM IN THE HALLWAY.

"DON'T SAY HELLO," HE CALLED OUT.

I GRUNTED SOMETHING IN RETURN.

HIS SMILE DISAPPEARED. "HEY, ARE YOU ALL RIGHT?"

"FINE. COOL."

"NO, YOU'RE NOT. NOT WITH THAT LOOK."

WHERE DID THIS GUY GET OFF? "WITH _WHAT_ LOOK?" I SNAPPED. "YOU DON'T EVEN KNOW ME."

"WHOA, SORRY. JUST TRYING TO HELP."

I TOOK A DEEP BREATH. I WAS TOO WOUND UP. "IT'S . . . NOTHING."

"LOOK," DUCKY SAID, "IF YOU EVER WANT TO TALK . . . I'M HERE, YOU KNOW."

I COULDN'T BELIEVE HE WASN'T FURIOUS AT ME. I THANKED HIM AND STARTED TO WALK AWAY -- AND HE WAS SMILING AT ME.

SMILING.

SUDDENLY I REALIZED SOMETHING. I REALLY _COULD_ TAKE HIM UP ON HIS OFFER.

I SPUN AROUND. "DUCKY?" I CALLED OUT. "CAN I ASK YOU SOME . . . GUY ADVICE?"

DUCKY FACED ME AND SHRUGGED. "WELL, I'M

NOT SURE I KNOW WHAT GUYS THINK. BUT I'LL
TRY."

"OKAY. SAY YOU'RE A HIGH SCHOOL SENIOR WHO
RAN AWAY FROM HOME? AND YOU'RE JUST BUMMING
YOUR WAY ACROSS THE COUNTRY AND YOU'RE
HANGING OUT AT THE BEACH? AND YOU MEET THIS
GIRL --"

"WHO JUST HAPPENS TO BE THIRTEEN AND
GOES TO VISTA?"

"DON'T INTERRUPT. ANYWAY, THE TWO OF YOU
ARE SO ALIKE IT'S NOT EVEN FUNNY. EXCEPT FOR
ONE THING. SHE BLABS EVERYTHING TO YOU, BUT
YOU'RE QUIET AND YOU LIKE TO BE ALONE, SO YOU
DON'T TELL HER MUCH. NOT EVEN YOUR LAST
NAME."

"SO FAR I DON'T LIKE THE SOUND OF THIS."

"I SEE HIM ALMOST EVERY TIME I GO TO THE
BEACH, DUCKY. HE SEEMS TO LIKE BEING WITH ME.
WE BLADE TOGETHER ON THE BOARDWALK. WE SIT
AT THE CAFE AND JOKE ABOUT THE WEIGHT
LIFTERS. HE EVEN LET ME TEACH HIM TO SURF."

"I DON'T KNOW . . ." DUCKY SIGHED. "I MEAN,
IF THE GUY DIDN'T LIKE YOU, HE WOULDN'T BE
THERE EVERY TIME YOU GO. CHANCES ARE HE WANTS
TO SEE YOU TOO."

"YOU THINK SO?"

Ducky shrugged. "Don't you?"

My heart was pumping. I thanked Ducky, kissed him on the cheek and ran toward my locker.

His words made sense. Carson must feel something for me. But how could I know for sure?

Well, I was going to make him tell me.

When the bell rang for the next period, I was out the door.

Lots of kids were outside for a recess, and no one noticed me leaving the school and heading for the bus stop.

A bus was pulling up as I arrived. It got me to Venice Beach by 1:00.

It took me about ten minutes to find Carson. He was sitting on a bench, reading a paperback. He did kind of a double take when he saw me. "Hey, where have you been? This is about the time you leave."

"I just got here," I replied. "I cut school in the middle of the day."

Carson looked amused. "Not bad."

I sat down next to him. "You missed me, huh?"

"Well, I --" Carson angled himself away, his face turning red.

"So, you want my address and phone number?"

"Huh? Well, I don't have a pen --"

"I do." I began unhooking my backpack. "I'll write it down. You have to give me yours too."

"Whoa, wait a minute. I can't do that. I don't have an address or number."

I grabbed some paper and a pen and began writing. "Then call me sometime. I won't mind."

"Okay. Whatever." I gave him the sheet and he scanned it quickly. "Where's Palo City?"

"Closer to Anaheim than here."

"Far, huh?"

"The bus is cheap. Want to come with me? My treat."

What was I saying?

Carson laughed. "No, thanks. Maybe another time."

"Carson, now that I've given you that, will you at least level with me?"

"I always do."

"Okay, then I want to know your last name. That's all. I mean --"

"Frame."

"We do know each other, and --" Screech went the brakes in my mind. "Frame? That's it? Carson Frame?"

"It's Albert Carson Frame on my birth certificate," Carson said. "And you?"

Oh my lord. I could not believe I hadn't told him. "Winslow!"

"Cool," Carson said with a shrug. "Was I right?"

"About what?"

"About names. They don't matter, do they?"

I must have been grinning like a fool, because my cheeks hurt. "Nahh, not at all."

I'm riding home now. I feel about ten pounds lighter. I think I may levitate off the seat.

Ducky was right. Carson had been waiting for me. Waiting for me at the beach, waiting for me to make a move.

And I did it. I broke the ice.

IN ONE SHORT TRIP, EVERYTHING HAS CHANGED.
ALBERT CARSON FRAME IS WRONG. WAY
WRONG. NAMES MATTER. A LOT.

WITHOUT A NAME, YOU'RE A PHANTOM. CARSON
AND I COULD HAVE DRIFTED IN AND OUT OF EACH
OTHER'S LIVES UNTIL SOMEDAY WE FLOATED APART
FOREVER.

NOW WE'RE REAL. REAL PEOPLE WITH REAL
IDENTITIES. NO MORE SECRETS. NO MORE CLOSED
DOORS.

I TRUST CARSON NOW. TOTALLY.

WEDNESDAY NIGHT

I HAVE TO WRITE THIS FAST.

I AM COLD. I CAN BARELY SEE THE PAGE. I
SHOULD HAVE BROUGHT A FLASHLIGHT WITH ME, BUT
IT'S TOO LATE FOR THAT NOW.

A CAR JUST DROVE BY AND SOMEONE SCREAMED
AT ME OUT THE WINDOW. I COULDN'T MAKE OUT
THE WORDS, AND I'M GLAD.

WHAT AM I DOING?

I KNOW WHAT I'M DOING. I HAVE JUST MADE
THE BIGGEST DECISION IN MY LIFE. I CAN'T
SECOND-GUESS IT NOW.

It all started this afternoon. When Dawn yelled at me.

Well, she had a reason to. She saw the beach towel sticking out of my pack as I walked past her house, on the way home from the bus stop.

"Your mom was in the hospital," she said, "and you were at the beach?"

Ugh. My secret was blown. But I was more concerned about Mom. I mean, she had been home when I left.

"She's in the hospital?" I asked.

Well, Dawn just started ranting. I have never seen her so mad. First she explained that Mom was in for tests — nothing major — but that Dad had been waiting for me in his car after school. When Dawn couldn't find me, she guessed that I was on a late field trip.

"I covered for you, Sunny!" she yelled. "Now I'm a liar, just like you! I hope you're happy."

"I wasn't lying!" I replied. "I never said I wasn't at the beach!"

"I am not hearing this. This is not Sunny Winslow speaking. What is with you, Sunny?

You're like a different person. I don't even know you anymore."

"No, you don't!"

I couldn't talk to her. I was worried about Mom. I was worried about Dad. I was worried about me.

Dawn, frankly, was way down on the priority list.

And she wasn't helping her cause by screaming at me.

"Fine!" she said. "Turn your back on your best friends. Keep secrets. Just don't expect us to hang around for long."

I was seeing red. "This is not about you, Dawn! You know, I have a point of view too!"

"Then tell it to me someday! But in the meantime, think about your mom and dad, Sunny. At least you can be loyal to them."

"I am loyal! They're the ones who don't even know I'm alive!"

"How can you even say that?"

Dawn was shaking her head in disbelief. I caught a glimpse of her earrings. They were shaped like big eyes with long lashes. I'd seen them before somewhere.

AND I KNEW WHERE.

SUDDENLY I FORGOT ABOUT OUR ARGUMENT. "WHERE'D YOU GET THOSE EARRINGS?" I ASKED.

"YOUR MOTHER GAVE THEM TO ME!" DAWN SHOT BACK.

I JUST STARTED SPUTTERING. "BUT -- WHY --?"

"MAYBE SHE'S HAPPY SOMEONE CARES ABOUT HER!"

WITH THAT, DAWN STORMED TOWARD HER HOUSE.

I FELT AS IF I'D BEEN PUNCHED IN THE STOMACH.

STILL DO.

NOW MOM'S GIVING HER FAMILY HEIRLOOMS TO DAWN? SINCE WHEN HAS DAWN BECOME THE DAUGHTER? WHY DOESN'T SHE JUST MOVE IN? THEN SHE MIGHT EVEN BE WRITTEN INTO THE WILL.

THIS IS MY REWARD FOR ALL THE HOSPITAL VISITS, ALL THE WORK AT DAD'S STORE, ALL THE SHOPPING AND CLEANING. I FINALLY DO A FEW THINGS FOR MYSELF, AND BLINK -- I'M OUT OF SIGHT, OUT OF MIND. REPLACED BY MY BEST FRIEND.

A PHANTOM. THAT'S WHAT I AM. A PHANTOM IN MY OWN FAMILY.

After Dawn left, I marched across our lawn, let myself into the empty house, and stomped upstairs to my room.

I went right to the closet and pulled out the antique music box. Raising it high over my head, I threw it.

It hit the floor with a loud crack. The wood shattered. Springs flew against the wall. The ugly little porcelain ballerina spun through the air and landed facedown at my feet.

I did the first thing that popped into my head. I stepped on her.

When I lifted my foot, her arms and legs were broken off at odd angles, leaving tiny dust piles at her shoulders and hips.

Ballerina, R.I.P. Ignored, stepped on, broken.

Like me.

That was when I made my decision.

It was clear as day. I had no other choice.

Which is why I am here at the bus stop again. For the last time.

I am going, going, gone. Packed up and

READY. I HAVE MY TOOTHBRUSH, MY SOAP, AND MY
BLADES. I LEFT MOM AND DAD A NOTE. I'LL BET
DAD DOESN'T EVEN NOTICE IT UNTIL TOMORROW.

WHO CARES? BY THEN I'LL BE FAR AWAY.

FROM THIS DAY ON, I AM ON THE ROAD.

AND I WILL NOT LOOK BACK.

WEDNESDAY NIGHT

I AM WRITING THIS AT A TABLE IN JAVA
VOOM. I HAVEN'T ORDERED ANYTHING, BUT THE
STAFF DOESN'T SEEM TO MIND.

I AM EXHAUSTED AND HUNGRY. I'VE JUST
SEARCHED THE BEACH FOR CARSON. I BLADED
PRACTICALLY ALL THE WAY TO SANTA MONICA.
I DIDN'T FIND HIM.

CARSON SAID HE DIDN'T HAVE A PHONE NUMBER
OR ADDRESS. I WONDER WHAT THAT MEANS. DOES
HE SLEEP ON THE BEACH? UNDER THE PIER?

THE SUN HAS SET. SOON IT'LL BE NIGHTTIME.

WHAT DO I DO NOW?

I CAN'T BELIEVE WHAT TIME IT IS. AND WHERE I'VE BEEN. AND WHAT HAS HAPPENED IN MY LIFE DURING THE LAST FEW HOURS.

I HAVE TO WRITE THIS DOWN. EVEN IF IT TAKES ME ALL NIGHT.

WHEN I LAST WROTE IN THIS JOURNAL, SITTING AT JAVA VOOM, I WAS ON THE VERGE OF TEARS. I WAS ALSO STARVING.

I CHECKED MY WALLET. STUPIDLY, I HAD NOT PACKED MUCH CASH. I SCANNED THE MENU, CHECKING THE PRICES.

"LOOKING FOR WHAT'S-HIS-NAME?" ASKED THE WAITER.

AT FIRST I ASSUMED HE WAS TALKING TO SOMEONE ELSE. BUT HIS EYES WERE ON ME. "EXCUSE ME?" I SAID.

"THE GUY YOU'RE ALWAYS WITH. HE WAS IN HERE AWHILE AGO."

"REALLY? DID YOU SEE WHERE HE WENT?"

"HE WENT TO THE CASHIER AND TRADED SOME BILLS FOR QUARTERS. EITHER HE'S DOING LAUNDRY OR HE'S AT THE ARCADE."

"THANKS!"

I took off down the boardwalk. The arcade was a blaze of garish light in the darkness. It was crowded. As I walked in, the beeps and sirens and explosions were deafening.

Carson was working a video game all the way in the back. I watched over his shoulder. When he saw me, he did a double take. "Heyyy, have you played this?"

I hadn't. I don't even remember the name of the game. But it doesn't matter. I was so relieved to see Carson.

I tried playing, but I was a total wimp, which made both of us laugh. Fortunately, Carson ran out of quarters, so we took a walk.

The moon was low and swollen. Its reflection on the water was like a trail of fire to the horizon.

I remember every word of what we said. I'll never forget it.

First, Carson put his arm around me. "Cold, huh?"

"I don't mind," I replied.

"What are you doing here at night?"

"I thought you'd never ask. I ran away."

Carson stopped walking. "You what?"

"RAN AWAY," I REPEATED. "LIKE YOU. I COULDN'T TAKE IT."

"OH." CARSON RAISED HIS EYEBROWS AND EXHALED. "UH, MAYBE WE SHOULD SIT DOWN."

THIS WAS NOT THE REACTION I EXPECTED. I THOUGHT HE'D BE HAPPY. OR EVEN AMUSED.

WAS _HE_ GOING TO LECTURE ME NOW TOO?

WE WALKED BACK INTO JAVA VOOM. THE WAITER SPOTTED ME AND GAVE ME A THUMBS-UP. CARSON ORDERED COFFEE AND A SANDWICH. I ORDERED A MUFFIN AND HOT CHOCOLATE.

AS THE WAITER RAN OFF, CARSON ASKED, "ARE YOU SURE YOU WANT TO DO THIS?"

"IF I SPENT ONE MORE MINUTE IN THAT HOUSE, I WOULD HAVE BROKEN EVERY WINDOW," I REPLIED. "I _HAVE_ TO RUN AWAY, CARSON. I HAVE NO CHOICE. I CAN'T BE TIED DOWN TO THEM ANYMORE."

HE NODDED. "I KNOW WHAT YOU MEAN. PEOPLE AREN'T MEANT TO LIVE IN ONE PLACE FOR A LONG TIME. THE IDEA OF A PERMANENT HOME AND STUFF -- IT'S ONLY A FEW HUNDRED YEARS OLD. FOR MILLIONS OF YEARS BEFORE THAT, PEOPLE TRAVELED ALL THE TIME. WE'RE PROGRAMMED TO."

"UH-HUH. YOU'RE DOING IT, AND YOU'RE HAPPY."

"I SEE ALL KINDS OF COOL PLACES. I'M

thinking of going south to Mexico, and then maybe work my way down to the Panama Canal."

"I've always wanted to go there!"

"But I might go the other way too. I hear the Badlands of South Dakota are totally awesome. And Montana has these huge ranches where you can get a job working with horses. But I also might want to check out this creative writing school in Iowa, where you can meet famous authors and maybe learn to write like Kerouac. I mean, cool or what?"

It was more than cool. It sounded like paradise to me. "Can I come with you?"

Carson smiled. "Yeah, right."

The waiter appeared with our orders, and I fell silent. When he was out of earshot, I leaned into the table and said, "I'm serious, Carson."

Carson's smile vanished. "Who-o-oa. Sunny, you can't -- I mean, I thought -- how do you expect --"

"I don't have a lot of money. But I can work too. And I'm really good at buying stuff cheaply --"

"Look, I know you're angry and all, but --"

"You're running away. I'm running away. It's perfect. We can keep each other company."

"But I don't want company, Sunny. I mean, no offense, but that's the whole point. You run away to be unattached. Not to tie yourself down."

"A family is tying yourself down -- a house, a school, a town. But this is different! We're exactly alike, Carson. I want to see the same things, go to the same places. We'll be able to share stuff, help each other when we're sick --"

"Sunny, how old are you?" Carson interrupted.

Gulp. "I'llbefourteenthisyear but what I'm trying to say is --"

"Wait a minute. You're thirteen?"

Why, why did he have to complicate this? "I said I'll be fourteen --"

"Sunny, whoa, hold it. Have you really thought about this? I mean, is your life that bad?"

I swallowed deeply. I'd been keeping the whole truth from Carson, and I was determined not to do it anymore.

I TOLD HIM EVERYTHING -- ABOUT MOM'S LUNG CANCER, THE CHEMOTHERAPY, THE RADIATION TREATMENTS, THE HAIR FALLOUT, THE SICKNESSES, THE TESTS, THE SCARES, THE TRIPS TO THE HOSPITAL. ABOUT THE ANNOYING SUPPORT GROUP. ABOUT DAD'S BUSINESS PROBLEMS AND HIS WORKAHOLISM. ABOUT ALL THE FAMILY FIGHTS AND MY SECRET IDENTITY AS ROBO SLAVE DAUGHTER. ABOUT MY SO-CALLED FRIENDS WHO HAD TURNED ON ME.

CARSON SIPPED HIS COFFEE. HE DIDN'T LOOK AT ME. HE DIDN'T SAY A WORD OR EVEN NOD. BUT I COULD TELL HE WAS LISTENING INTENTLY.

WHEN I WAS DONE, MY CHEEKS WERE STREAKED WITH TEARS AND MY VOICE WAS HOARSE. I FELT COLD AND VULNERABLE, AS IF A LAYER OF SKIN HAD BEEN STRIPPED FROM ME.

HE HANDED ME A PAPER NAPKIN. "YOU NEED THIS. WANT SOMETHING ELSE TO EAT?"

"IS THAT ALL YOU CAN SAY?" I EXPLODED. "I JUST TOLD YOU THE STORY OF MY LIFE. DO YOU THINK THAT WAS EASY? DIDN'T YOU HEAR A WORD OF IT?"

"LET ME GET THIS STRAIGHT, SUNNY. YOU HAVE A MOM AND DAD. THEY'RE STILL MARRIED AND THEY BOTH CARE ABOUT YOU."

"But —"

"But they're real busy. Your mom has cancer, and your dad's having business problems. So they can't see you, and that makes you angry. But you have these really close friends. You see them all the time. When you started skipping school, they got on your case. Because they care about you too." Carson shook his head in disbelief. "And you want to run away from all that?"

"You don't get it, do you? Carson, my life is a mess. It's falling apart. I can't sleep at night. No one sees me for who I am. I have to run away. And if you're not going with me, I'll go by myself. And I better go now before they chase after me and try to drag me back. I thought you, of all people, would understand, but I guess you don't."

"I understand," Carson said, almost under his breath. "It's a tough thing. I feel bad for you. I feel bad for your mom and dad too. But think about it. You have people who want you back. If I had what you have, I'd never have left home in the first place."

"What I have?" I shot back. "Puh-leeze. Oh, I guess I'm wrong. My life is just a

PARADISE. WHY DID YOU LEAVE HOME, CARSON? WHAT MAKES YOU SO DIFFERENT? SO -- SO SUPERIOR?"

CARSON GLARED AT ME. WITHOUT SAYING A WORD, HE STOOD UP AND WALKED TOWARD THE EXIT.

"WAIT!" I CALLED OUT, RUNNING AFTER HIM. "WHERE ARE YOU GOING? I -- I WANT TO LISTEN! TALK TO ME, CARSON!"

CARSON SPUN AROUND. "SUNNY, DO YOU HAVE A MOTTO?"

"A MOTTO?"

"LIKE, FOR YOURSELF. FOR LIFE."

"NO . . ."

"YOU KNOW WHAT MINE IS? DON'T COMPLAIN; DON'T EXPLAIN. IT'S THE ONLY USEFUL THING I EVER REMEMBER MY DAD SAYING. I TRY TO LIVE BY IT. IT MAKES ME HAPPY. WELL, I'VE ALREADY BROKEN BOTH RULES. CONSIDER YOURSELF LUCKY."

"SO YOU DO HAVE A FAMILY!" I EXCLAIMED. "TELL ME ABOUT THEM, CARSON! DID SOMETHING BAD HAPPEN? I MEAN, YOU DON'T HAVE TO TELL ME THE DETAILS IF YOU DON'T WANT . . ."

CARSON'S FACE WAS DARKENING. I COULD SEE HIS JAW MUSCLES WORKING. I BRACED MYSELF FOR A BIG, ANGRY BLAST.

BUT ALL HE SAID WAS, "'BYE, SUNNY."

Before I could reply, he was out the door.

I lunged forward to go after him. I opened the door and stepped onto the boardwalk.

The night crowd had arrived, full force. The boardwalk was practically shoulder to shoulder with people. Carson was somewhere in there, swallowed up and moving fast.

I stood there, frozen, trying to hold back a scream that was welling up inside me.

I felt a tap on my shoulder. I turned quickly.

The waiter was standing behind me, holding out a bill. "Excuse me?" he said. "Will you be leaving your table?"

"Uh . . . yeah." I took a look at the bill, then dug around for money in my pocket.

I had enough to cover, with a little to spare. I gave the waiter what I had.

"Will you be needing change?" he asked.

"Okay," I replied.

His eyes widened. "You will?"

A tip. I had to leave a tip. "Uh, no. Keep it."

Boy, did he give me a nasty look.

FRANKLY, I SHOULD HAVE GIVEN A LOOK BACK TO HIM. HE HAD ALMOST ALL MY MONEY NOW. I WAS BROKE.

BROKE, ALONE, AND HOMELESS.

I FELT AS IF THE FLOOR HAD JUST DROPPED AWAY FROM MY FEET AND I WAS PLUNGING INTO BLACKNESS.

SUDDENLY, RUNNING AWAY SEEMED LIKE A MAJORLY DUMB IDEA.

I GRABBED THE BUS SCHEDULE OUT OF MY POCKET. I FOLLOWED THE DEPARTURE SCHEDULE DOWN TO THE FINAL LISTING.

WHICH WAS RIGHT THEN.

MY BACKPACK WAS STILL IN THE CAFE. I RAN INSIDE AND SCOOPED IT OFF THE FLOOR. THEN I BOLTED FOR THE BUS STOP.

I COULD SEE A BUS WAITING, ITS ENGINE RUNNING. "WAAAAAAIIT!" I SCREAMED, FLAILING MY ARMS.

VRRRRRROOOM! THE BUS ANSWERED.

IT PULLED AWAY BEFORE I REACHED THE STOP.

A MAN IN A DRIVER'S UNIFORM WAS STANDING THERE, LOOKING AT ME BLANKLY.

"WHEN'S THE NEXT BUS?" I ASKED.

"FIVE A.M. TOMORROW," HE ANSWERED.

BIG HELP.

I SPOTTED A PAY PHONE NEARBY. I FISHED IN MY POCKET FOR CHANGE.

ONE QUARTER. PERIOD.

(I SHOULDN'T HAVE TIPPED THAT WAITER, AFTER ALL.)

I DROPPED THE QUARTER IN THE PHONE AND PUNCHED IN MY NUMBER.

"HELLO, YOU HAVE REACHED THE WINSLOW RESIDENCE," SAID MY VOICE. "WE CAN'T COME TO THE PHONE RIGHT NOW . . ."

I HUNG UP. WHAT COULD I SAY? "MOM AND DAD, I CHANGED MY MIND ABOUT RUNNING AWAY, SO WHEN YOU GET IN, COULD YOU PICK ME UP AT VENICE BEACH?"

NO WAY.

I TURNED BACK TOWARD THE BEACH. MUSIC WAS BLARING FROM ONE OF THE SHOPS. PEOPLE WERE MILLING AROUND, SHOPPING, TALKING.

MAYBE THINGS WOULDN'T BE SO BAD, AFTER ALL. MAYBE VENICE BEACH STAYS LIKE THIS ALL NIGHT. MAYBE I COULD CAMP ON A BENCH, OR ON THE SAND. MAYBE LOTS OF PEOPLE DO THE SAME THING.

I WALKED SLOWLY ALONG THE BOARDWALK, REMEMBERING THE HOURS CARSON AND I HAD SPENT BLADING. I PASSED THE AREA WHERE WE'D

FALLEN INTO THE SAND, LAUGHING. I LOOKED OUT AT THE JETTY WHERE HE'D REMOVED THE SPLINTER FROM MY TOE.

By THE TIME I REACHED THE ARCADE, I WAS A WRECK.

I HURRIED TO A MORE SECLUDED SPOT, FAR AWAY FROM THE ARCADE RACKET. UNDER A TALL STREETLIGHT, I SAT ON AN EMPTY BENCH.

CARSON'S WORDS CAME BACK TO ME: <u>My MOM PROBABLY JUST DISCOVERED I'M GONE. HER BOYFRIEND'S THRILLED, I'LL BET. . . . YOU HAVE PEOPLE WHO WANT YOU BACK. IF I HAD WHAT YOU HAVE, I'D NEVER HAVE LEFT HOME IN THE FIRST PLACE . . .</u>

I HADN'T REALLY LISTENED TO HIM. I WAS SO BUSY COMPLAINING, I HADN'T UNDERSTOOD WHAT HE WAS TRYING TO TELL ME.

WHATEVER HAD HAPPENED TO HIM MUST HAVE BEEN AWFUL. JUDGING FROM HIS REACTION, IT MADE MY LIFE LOOK ROSY.

I FELT LIKE A FAKE. A WHINING, TAGALONG, CHICKEN-HEARTED FAKE. THE MOMENT CARSON DISAPPEARED INTO THE DARKNESS, WHAT WAS THE FIRST THING I DID? HEAD FOR THE BUS HOME.

HOME TO MY NICE, NORMAL LIFE.

WHAT IF I HAD MADE THAT BUS? I THOUGHT

ABOUT HOW I'D HAVE TO EXPLAIN MYSELF TO DAD,
WHO WAS PROBABLY JUST COMING HOME FROM WORK,
SWEATY AND MISERABLE. I THOUGHT ABOUT
TOMORROW -- SCHOOL, A HOSPITAL VISIT, FOOD
SHOPPING, LAUNDRY, PROBABLY A FEW ARGUMENTS
ALONG THE WAY WITH DAWN, MAGGIE, AND MY
TEACHERS.

IT ALL MADE MY STOMACH TURN.

I WAS FURIOUS AT CARSON. WAS? I AM.
WITH HIM, I COULD HAVE RUN AWAY. HE'S OLDER,
HE KNOWS HIS WAY AROUND, HE HAS MORE JOB
SKILLS.

WITHOUT HIM, I'M REALLY IN TROUBLE.

HOW DARE HE LEAVE ME LIKE THAT? HOW DARE
HE JUDGE MY PROBLEMS AND DECIDE I'M NOT
WORTH HIS COMPANY?

HOW DARE HE MAKE ME FEEL LIKE A FAKE?

MAYBE HIS PROBLEMS ARE WORSE, BUT THAT
DOESN'T MAKE MINE LESS IMPORTANT. MY ANGER
AND DISGUST, ALL THE PRESSURE I'M FEELING --
THEY'RE REAL. I AM SICK OF MY LIFE. SICK OF MY
MOTHER BEING SICK. SICK OF MY DAD'S DEMANDS.
SICK OF NOT BEING UNDERSTOOD BY EVERYONE,
INCLUDING CARSON.

IF THOSE FEELINGS ARE FAKE, THEN WHY AM I
HERE? WHY AM I SO UNHAPPY?

A couple passed by, eating ice-cream cones and giggling to each other. I felt hungry again. And lonely.

A gust of ocean breeze made my skin prickle. I left the bench and began walking.

And walking.

By midnight I was still walking. But not too many others were. The crowd had cleared. The shops were closing up.

Suddenly Venice Beach wasn't looking so friendly.

The sand was a dull bone-white in the moonlight, all mottled with footprints. Little piles of rocks and trash jutted up here and there, like underground creatures emerging. A few stragglers walked slowly by, stopping to pick things up.

Panic. Blind panic. I was going to have to sleep here? Alone and out in the open?

As I walked along, I caught sight of a tall sign I'd never noticed. In big letters it read NO CAMPING, NO FIRES, NO SLEEPING.

Great.

The wind had picked up, and I was

SHIVERING. I LOOKED AROUND FRANTICALLY. JU[ST TO]
MY LEFT WAS AN ELEVATED PIER. IT BEGAN [AT]
THE BOARDWALK AND CONTINUED OUT OVER THE
SAND AND INTO THE OCEAN. IT WAS SUPPORTED
UNDERNEATH BY ARCHED COLUMNS.

IF I SLEPT UNDER THERE, WHO COULD SEE
ME? IT WOULD BE PRIVATE. IT WOULD ALSO BE A
WARMER SHELTER, SHIELDED FROM THE WIND.

THAT WAS WHEN I HEARD THE FOOTSTEPS
BEHIND ME. I STOPPED AND LOOKED AROUND.

A MAN WAS WINDOW-SHOPPING. AT A STORE
THAT HAD CLOSED.

I WALKED AGAIN, A LITTLE FASTER. THE
FOOTSTEPS STARTED AGAIN.

I LOOKED OVER MY SHOULDER AND SAW THE
SAME MAN. HE WAS LIT FROM BEHIND, AND ALL I
COULD MAKE OUT WAS A BLACK LEATHER JACKET
AND LONG, STRINGY HAIR.

I STOPPED AGAIN. SO DID HE.

I TOOK OFF AT A DEAD RUN. I DUCKED INTO
THE NEAREST OPEN STORE, AN OLD-FASHIONED FIVE-
AND-DIME. QUICKLY I DARTED THROUGH THE AISLES
UNTIL I WAS ALL THE WAY IN THE BACK. I PULLED
SOMETHING OFF THE SHELF, PRETENDING TO BE
SHOPPING.

"MAY I HELP YOU?" A VOICE ASKED.

I NEARLY JUMPED. I TURNED TO SEE A SHORT, BALDING MAN WEARING A NAME TAG.

"OH . . . JUST LOOKING."

"WHAT SIZE MEN'S BRIEFS DO YOU NEED?"

YIKES. SO THAT'S WHAT I WAS HOLDING. I TOSSED THEM BACK.

THEN I SAW THE MAN AGAIN.

HE WAS IN THE NEXT AISLE, LOOKING THROUGH THE SHELVES, BUSILY MOVING THINGS AROUND. I COULD SEE NOW THAT THE JACKET WAS BLACK FABRIC, NOT LEATHER. HIS HAIR WAS PULLED BACK INTO A PONYTAIL NOW TOO, BUT HE DIDN'T FOOL ME.

I LEANED CLOSE TO THE CLERK. "UM, DO YOU KNOW THAT GUY?" I WHISPERED, GESTURING TOWARD THE MAN.

THE CLERK GLANCED OVER WITHOUT MOVING HIS HEAD. "NO. MAY I HELP YOU?"

"NO! UH, WELL, THANKS, BUT I HAVE TO GO."

I FLEW OUT OF THERE. I SCANNED THE BOARDWALK AND SAW A FEW LONELY FIGURES, BUT I DIDN'T STOP FOR A CLOSER LOOK.

I HEADED STRAIGHT FOR THE PIER AND DUCKED UNDER THE NEAREST ARCH.

It was pitch-black. I felt around until I touched the cement wall. It was cold and clammy, but I sat against it, panting for breath.

Tears were cascading down my face. I felt like a prisoner on the lam. How was I going to make it through the night? What if rats lived under the pier? Crabs? Kidnappers?

Calm down, Sunny. Think.

Okay. All I had to do was stay still. If I couldn't sleep, so what? I could keep my eyes open all night and nap in the morning, when it was safer.

Then, when I was rested, I'd have to make a plan. Maybe I could lie about my age and find a job. I could serve coffee at Java Voom. Save enough money and travel to Mexico or South Dakota.

The sound of a car engine broke the stillness, followed by the crackling of a two-way radio. I peeked out of the darkness and looked toward the boardwalk.

A police car had pulled to a stop.

I ducked back. Oh. My. God. They were after me. Dad had sent a dragnet out.

I FROZE. I TRIED NOT TO MAKE A SOUND.

AFTER A FEW MOMENTS I PEEKED BACK OUT AGAIN.

I SAW TWO POLICE OFFICERS EMERGING FROM A CONVENIENCE STORE. ONE WAS CARRYING A BOX OF DONUTS, AND THE OTHER HELD TWO CAPPED PAPER CUPS. THEY STARTED LAUGHING AND CLIMBED INTO THE CAR, WHICH CONTINUED CRUISING DOWN THE BOARDWALK.

I LET OUT A DEEP BREATH AND SANK BACK AGAINST THE WALL. MY ENERGY WAS GONE. MY EYELIDS WERE DROOPING. A DREAM WAS STARTING TO SEEP INTO MY BRAIN . . .

SCRITCH . . . SCRITCH . . .

MY EYES SPRANG OPEN. THE SOUND WAS TO MY LEFT. DEEPER INTO THE BLACKNESS.

I SQUINTED. MY VISION HAD ADJUSTED ABOUT AS MUCH AS IT COULD, AND I TRIED TO FOCUS ON A COUPLE OF SMALL, DISTANT SHADOWS. BUT THEY WEREN'T MOVING.

I LEANED BACK AGAIN AND STAYED ROCK STILL. LISTENING. HEARING NOTHING BUT THE SOFT LAPPING OF THE WAVES.

SNAP!

A SUDDEN FLARE OF LIGHT. TO MY LEFT.

I FROZE.

A match was flickering about three feet away. In its amber light were two bloodshot eyes and a gap-toothed grin.

"Cigarette?"

The voice was like a slap. I bolted.

"POLICE!" I shrieked.

My shoes dug into the sand, slowing me down. I tried harder to run, but I bumped into something and fell. I rolled once and felt sand in my mouth and hair. Spitting and coughing, I scrambled to my feet.

I heard a burst of wild laughter. To my right, near the water, a man in a raggedy coat was doubled over, pointing at me.

Who were these people?

What was I doing here?

I heard a scream and realized it was me.

I was hysterical. Sand was in my eyes now. I ran blindly.

"EEEEEEEAAAAAAAAAAAAAGHHH!"

"Sunny?"

How did they know my name? They were calling me!

"Sunny!"

I stopped running. My heart felt like a jackhammer.

But I knew that voice.

"Over here!"

He was waving to me from the open door of a car in a small, deserted parking lot beyond the convenience store.

"Ducky?" I could barely get the word out of my parched throat.

Ducky was walking toward me now, a curious smile on his face. "What happened to you, girl?"

"Duckyyyyyy!" I practically tackled him to the sand. All I could do was hold him tightly and sob and sob.

"Sssshh," he said gently, wrapping his arms around me. "Are you okay?"

"I'm so glad you're here! It's horrible -- I was almost -- how did you find me?"

"I heard you screaming, and I said, 'Sunny?'"

"Not funny!" I said, laughing through my tears.

"I heard your parents have been worried sick. When your dad brought your mom home from the hospital tonight, they saw your note and freaked."

"M-my mom's ho-home?" I said, choking back sniffles.

"She was feeling okay, so the doctors let her go. Anyway, your dad called Dawn, and she called me. And I remembered what you said about meeting your boyfriend -- you mentioned something about a cafe, a boardwalk, and weight lifters." Ducky smiled. "I had a hunch."

"Th --" Sniff. "Thanks, Ducky."

"Well?" he said. "What now? Are we going home or running away?"

Ugh. Mom and Dad had told everyone about the note. If I went home now, I'd be explaining myself for months.

For a moment I considered asking Ducky for some money and walking off.

But that moment passed. At this point, the last thing I wanted was to be alone.

"Take me home," I said.

Ducky's cool. He called Mom and Dad from a pay phone and told them we were on our way. I didn't talk to them. I couldn't.

I fell asleep on the ride home. Ducky had

TO WAKE ME WHEN WE WERE IN FRONT OF MY
HOUSE.

I CLIMBED OUT AND WAVED GOOD-BYE AS HE
DROVE OFF. BUT I COULDN'T GO INSIDE. I
COULDN'T FACE THEM. NOT YET.

I TURNED AND WENT STRAIGHT TO DAWN'S. I
STOOD OUTSIDE HER WINDOW AND TOSSED PEBBLES
AT IT UNTIL A LIGHT BLINKED ON.

THE WINDOW OPENED. DAWN LOOKED SURPRISED.
RELIEVED A LITTLE. BUT DEFINITELY NOT PLEASED.
SHE DID COME TO THE FRONT DOOR, THOUGH, AND
SHE WASN'T SWINGING A BASEBALL BAT. THOSE WERE
GOOD SIGNS.

"HI," I SAID.

I THOUGHT SHE WAS GOING TO YELL AT ME,
BUT SHE DIDN'T. INSTEAD, SHE PUT HER ARMS
AROUND ME AND STARTED TO CRY, BLUBBERING
ABOUT HOW WORRIED SHE HAD BEEN.

IT FELT GOOD. REALLY GOOD.

FOR AWHILE.

WHEN WE WENT INSIDE HER HOUSE, THE FIRST
THING DAWN DID WAS CALL MOM AND DAD. SHE
HELD THE RECEIVER OUT TO ME.

"HELLO?" IT WAS DAD.

"HI, DAD, IT'S --"

Before I could say another word, Dad started gasping. I thought he was having a heart attack, but he was crying.

Mom picked up the other extension. She sounded breathy and tired. I told her I was at Dawn's, and she said, "Are you okay, sweetheart?"

I felt like a total worthless subhuman. Mom was up late, feeling horrible, all because of what I had done -- and she was asking me if I was okay!

I had let her down, big-time.

I opened my mouth, but all that came out was a strangled croak. And then tears were running down my cheeks.

"Shush, sweetie," Mom said tenderly, "it's okay. We'll talk it out when you come home. It's been tough for you. I understand . . ."

I was practically hiccuping my sobs now, but I managed to say good-bye. Dawn had found a box of tissues and set it before me.

I blew my nose and took a few deep breaths. "Sorry."

Dawn was shaking her head. "Sunny . . . why?"

It was a simple question. But just thinking about an answer was like preparing for a major war. I didn't have the energy to do it.

"Can we talk about it tomorrow?" I asked.

Dawn shrugged. "Okay. Sure. If that's what you want. I guess I'll walk you home."

No way. The thought of it turned me inside out. I could not face Mom and Dad. I couldn't stay up and answer their questions. I was ready to collapse.

I asked Dawn if I could spend the rest of the night on the living room sofa.

She puffed out her cheeks and exhaled. I knew she wanted to yell at me. I could see it in her eyes. And I wouldn't have blamed her if she did.

But all she said was, "You call your parents and tell them. I'll get a blanket. And you owe me an explanation, first thing in the morning."

Dawn has amazing self-control.

I nodded and promised to tell her everything. And I called Mom and Dad right away.

They're mad at me too. I just know it by their voices.

Tomorrow is going to be awful.

Thursday 11/6
Study hall

I was right.

Dawn was up at 7:00 this morning. She wanted to talk to me before her dad and Carol awoke.

I barely remember what I said. Just the basics, I guess. The way I was feeling, how I met Carson, what happened last night.

It must have sunk in, because Dawn was pretty nice to me. Not exactly warm and cuddly. Not exactly full of forgiveness. But concerned.

I'll take what I can get.

Going home afterward was the worst. If Dawn hadn't walked with me, I might have bolted for the bus stop.

But she did. And I didn't. And I had to face Mom and Dad. It was the hardest thing

I'VE EVER DONE. I TRIED TO BE HONEST. I TOLD THEM I FELT NEGLECTED. I TOLD THEM HOW TENSE AND AFRAID I'D BEEN. I EXPLAINED WHY I FOUND MOM'S "HEIRLOOMS" SO UPSETTING. AND I ADMITTED MY TRIPS TO VENICE BEACH.

WELL, NOT ALL OF THEM. AND I DIDN'T MENTION CARSON.

MOM AND DAD LISTENED GRAVELY. THE WHOLE THING WAS A BIG SHOCK TO THEM.

THEY REACTED KIND OF THE WAY I EXPECTED. DAD ASKED A FEW ANGRY QUESTIONS -- "WHY DIDN'T YOU TELL US?" AND "DON'T YOU THINK IT'S BEEN HARD FOR US TOO?" -- BUT MOSTLY THEY LISTENED. MOM EVEN COMFORTED ME.

"THINGS WILL BE BETTER," SHE SAID, "AS SOON AS I'M BACK TO NORMAL."

RIGHT.

THAT STATEMENT REALLY TURNED ME INSIDE OUT. I HAD TO FIGHT BACK TEARS.

NORMAL?

I COULD NOT TELL MOM WHAT I KNOW. NORMAL IS A THING OF THE PAST. I KNOW ENOUGH NOT TO EXPECT NORMAL ANYMORE.

SOMEHOW I MADE IT TO SCHOOL TODAY. BUT MY BRAIN IS PRETTY USELESS. DAWN IS STILL

ACTING WEIRD. MAGGIE ISN'T TALKING TO ME. ONLY DUCKY IS FRIENDLY.

So MY WORK IS CUT OUT FOR ME HERE.

SOMETIMES I WISH THIS WERE ALL ONE BIG STORY, AND THIS WERE THE HARD PART. THE MIDDLE, WHERE EVERYTHING GOES WRONG BEFORE EVERYTHING GOES RIGHT.

BUT IT'S NOT. AND HAPPY ENDINGS ARE FOR FAIRY TALES.

I WOULD NEVER, EVER TELL ANYONE THIS, BUT I'M SCARED.

REALLY SCARED.

AND I DESPERATELY WANT TO ESCAPE.

SOMEWHERE.

L. GODWIN

Ann M. Martin

About the Author

ANN MATTHEWS MARTIN was born on August 12, 1955. She grew up in Princeton, NJ, with her parents and her younger sister, Jane.

Although Ann used to be a teacher and then an editor of children's books, she's now a full-time writer. She gets the ideas for her books from many different places. Some are based on personal experiences. Others are based on childhood memories and feelings. Many are written about contemporary problems or events.

All of Ann's characters are made up. But some of her characters are based on real people. Sometimes Ann names her characters after people she knows, other times she chooses names she likes.

In addition to California Diaries, Ann Martin has written many other books, including the Baby-sitters Club series. She has written twelve novels for young people, including *Missing Since Monday, With You or Without You, Slam Book,* and *Just a Summer Romance.*

Ann M. Martin does not live in California, though she does visit frequently. She lives in New York with her cats, Gussie and Woody. Her hobbies are reading, sewing, and needlework — especially making clothes for children.

Look For #3

Maggie

Monday 12/1
7:38 P.M.

What have I done?

I am typing this at my desk, standing up.

I am standing up because I can turn and look at my image.

I am looking at my image because it may be the last time I see myself alive.

If I do not survive the day and someone reads this, I plead insanity. I had another grueling rehearsal and I was tired. So I did not know what I was doing afterward.

A half hour ago I was in the kitchen. I was stacking the dishwasher, pushing back the locks of hair that kept falling into my face, wishing I had gotten a haircut.

Then I was up here in my room, looking

at that hair. Looking at the nice, even, perfect, shoulder-length style. Hanging a little too long and a little limp, but still neat. Neat and nice.

I began imagining.

I pictured it gone. I tried to feel the breezes on my bare neck. On my ears.

My soul filled with happiness.

So I grabbed a pair of scissors from my desk.

I held out a strand. I opened the blades.

But my fingers stayed put.

I knew I could not do this. Not to my own hair. It was insane. Better idea: call Dawn and Sunny. Ask their advice. Have Ducky drive me to a hairstylist, at least. Someone must still be open.

Then I snapped the blade shut.

A clump of hair fell to my dresser table.

Perfect, blonde hair that spilled like a pile of straw.

Then I took another snip.

YOU READ THE BOOKS. NOW GET AWAY FROM IT ALL.

Enter the

California

Diaries

Getaway Sweepstakes

GRAND PRIZE: A California Getaway!
Now you and your friend can take off together to write your *own* California diary.

WIN A TRIP TO CALIFORNIA!

100 RUNNERS UP:
A signed copy of California Diaries Book #3: Maggie!

OFFICIAL RULES:

1. No purchase necessary. To enter fill out the coupon below or hand print your name, address, birth date (day/mo./year), and telephone number on a 3" x 5" card and mail with your original entry (must be under 100 words) to: California Diaries Getaway Sweepstakes, c/o Scholastic Inc., P.O. Box 7500, 2931 East McCarty Street, Jefferson City, MO 65102. Enter as often as you wish, one entry to an envelope. Each entry must be original. All entries must be postmarked by 10/10/97. Partially completed entries or mechanically reproduced entries will not be accepted. Sponsors assume no responsibility for lost, misdirected, damaged, stolen, postage-due, illegible or late entries. All entries become the property of the sponsor and will not be returned.

2. Sweepstakes open to residents of the USA no older than 15 as of 10/10/97, except employees of Scholastic Inc., and its respective affiliates, subsidiaries, respective advertising, promotion, and fulfillment agencies, and the immediate families of each. Sweepstakes is void where prohibited by law.

3. Winners will be selected at random on or about 10/24/97, by Scholastic Inc., whose decision is final. Odds of winning are dependent on the number of entries received. Except where prohibited, by accepting the prize, winner consents to the use of his/her name, age, entry, and/or likeness by sponsors for publicity purposes without further compensation. Winners will be notified by mail and will be required to sign and return an affidavit of eligibility and liability release within fourteen days of notification, or the prize will be forfeited and awarded to an alternate winner.

4. Prize: A three (3) day, two (2) night trip for three people (includes winner, a parent or guardian and one friend) to California (date and exact location of trip to be determined by sponsor on or about October 24, 1997). Includes round-trip coach, air transportation from airport nearest winner's home to California airport, two nights lodging and meals. Travel must include Saturday night stay. (Est. retail value of prize $2,500.)

5. Prize is non-transferable, not returnable, and cannot be sold or redeemed for cash. No substitutions allowed. All taxes on prize are the sole responsibility of the the winner. By accepting the prize, winner agrees that Scholastic Inc. and its respective officers, directors, agents and employees will have no liability or responsibility for any injuries, losses or damages or any kind resulting from the acceptance, possession or use of any prize and they will be held harmless against any claims of liability arising directly or indirectly from the prizes awarded.

6. For list of winners, send a self-addressed stamped envelope after 10/24/97 to California WINNERS, c/o Scholastic Inc., Trade Marketing Dept., 555 Broadway, New York, NY 10012.

YES! Enter me in the California Diaries Getaway Sweepstakes.

Name

Address

City   State   Zip

Send entry form to: California Diaries Getaway Sweepstakes, c/o Scholastic Inc., P.O. Box 7500, 2931 East McCarty Street, Jefferson City, MO 65102